Rival Angels

Art: Alan Evans
Story: Alan Evans and Justin Riley
Color Assists: Aaron Daly
Rival Angels created by
Alan Evans

www.RivalAngels.com

Rival Angels Season 3, Volume 1. ISBN 978-0-9827013-6-2.
Rival Angels and all associated characters and their distinct likenesses are © 2016-2017 of Alan Evans. The events presented in this book are entirely fictional. Any similarity to persons living or dead is purely coincidental. No portion of this comic book may be reproduced by any means (digital or print) without express permission, except for purposes of review.

RIVAL ANGELS
SEASON 3
CHAPTER 1

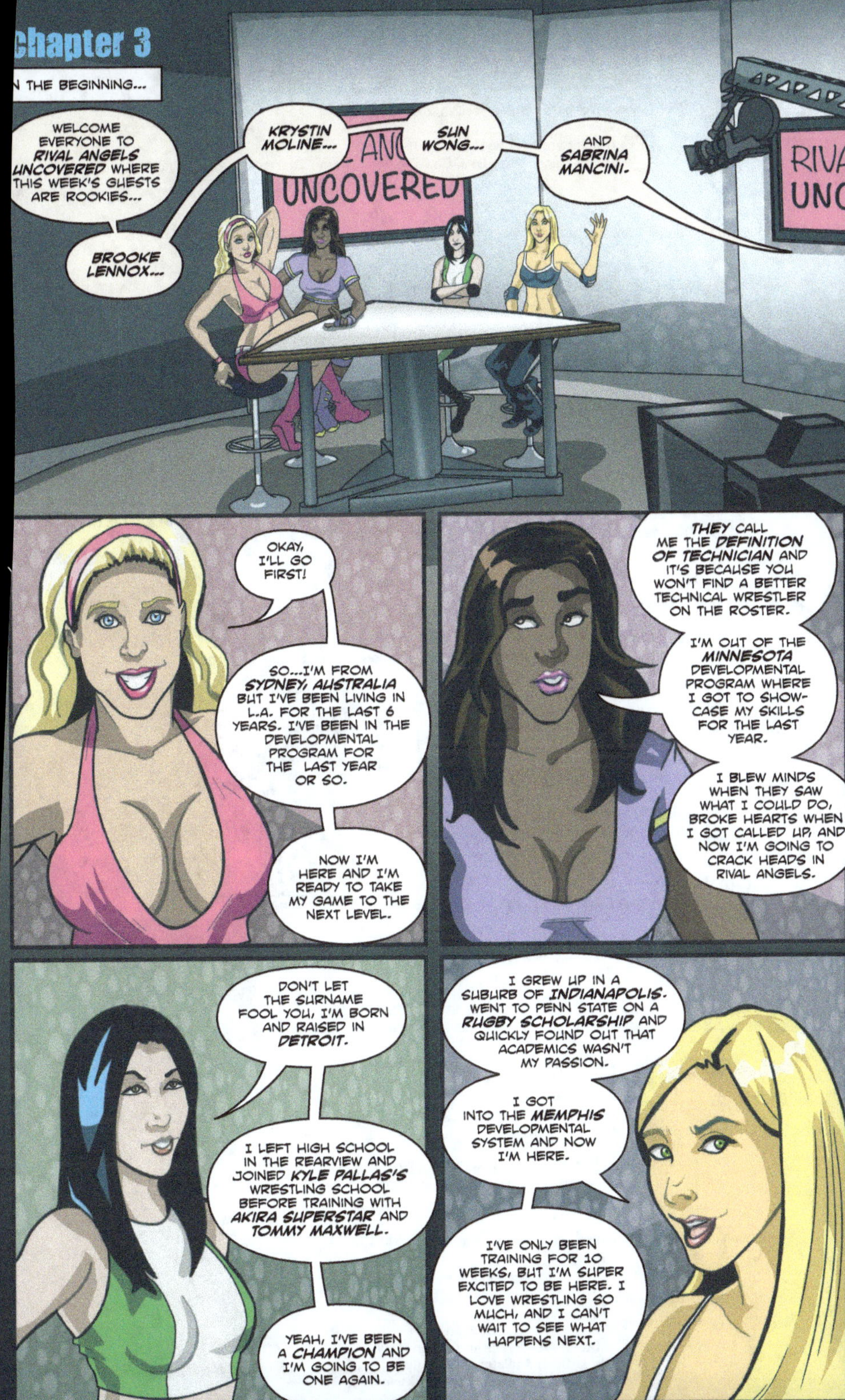
IN THE BEGINNING...
WELCOME EVERYONE TO RIVAL ANGELS UNCOVERED WHERE THIS WEEK'S GUESTS ARE ROOKIES...
KRYSTIN MOLINE...
SUN WONG...
AND SABRINA MANCINI.
BROOKE LENNOX...
UNCOVERED
RIVA
UNC
OKAY, I'LL GO FIRST!
SO...I'M FROM SYDNEY, AUSTRALIA BUT I'VE BEEN LIVING IN L.A. FOR THE LAST 6 YEARS. I'VE BEEN IN THE DEVELOPMENTAL PROGRAM FOR THE LAST YEAR OR SO.
NOW I'M HERE AND I'M READY TO TAKE MY GAME TO THE NEXT LEVEL.
THEY CALL ME THE DEFINITION OF TECHNICIAN AND IT'S BECAUSE YOU WON'T FIND A BETTER TECHNICAL WRESTLER ON THE ROSTER.
I'M OUT OF THE MINNESOTA DEVELOPMENTAL PROGRAM WHERE I GOT TO SHOWCASE MY SKILLS FOR THE LAST YEAR.
I BLEW MINDS WHEN THEY SAW WHAT I COULD DO, BROKE HEARTS WHEN I GOT CALLED UP, AND NOW I'M GOING TO CRACK HEADS IN RIVAL ANGELS.
DON'T LET THE SURNAME FOOL YOU, I'M BORN AND RAISED IN DETROIT.
I LEFT HIGH SCHOOL IN THE REARVIEW AND JOINED KYLE PALLAS'S WRESTLING SCHOOL BEFORE TRAINING WITH AKIRA SUPERSTAR AND TOMMY MAXWELL.
YEAH, I'VE BEEN A CHAMPION AND I'M GOING TO BE ONE AGAIN.
I GREW UP IN A SUBURB OF INDIANAPOLIS. WENT TO PENN STATE ON A RUGBY SCHOLARSHIP AND QUICKLY FOUND OUT THAT ACADEMICS WASN'T MY PASSION.
I GOT INTO THE MEMPHIS DEVELOPMENTAL SYSTEM AND NOW I'M HERE.
I'VE ONLY BEEN TRAINING FOR 10 WEEKS, BUT I'M SUPER EXCITED TO BE HERE. I LOVE WRESTLING SO MUCH, AND I CAN'T WAIT TO SEE WHAT HAPPENS NEXT.

 **Leo Tastic** * 2hr Ago   5: LIKE   REPLY
Brenda, the true champ really wrecked UltraFAIL!!! TABLES FTW!

 **HEY HOW R U** * 2hr Ago   8: LIKE   REPLY
Yeah, she's a real hero. What a positive role model.

Chick Hera * 1hr Ago 2: LIKE   REPLY
Wrong place, wrong time. Could've been anyone. Don't mess with the Irish!

 **CEEJ** * 3hr Ago   2: LIKE   REPLY
I heard Rua broke Mancini's back.

 **Kat's Tears** * 2hr Ago   8: LIKE   REPLY
LOL. That's the dumbest thing I've ever heard. She walked back on her own!

CEEJ * 2hr Ago   0: LIKE   REPLY
READ WHAT I WROTE. I didn't say she couldn't walk. smh

 **Zomaya** * 2hr Ago   1: LIKE   REPLY
 She could put me through a table. I'd take a side of Ultrakick too.

 **swapnil** * 2hr Ago   8: LIKE   REPLY
Loved Rua as champ but got stale. Looking forward to the Reign of Yvonne.

Mr. Logic * 1hr Ago   2: LIKE   REPLY
This defies logic. How many PPVs did she sell out? Every one of them.

 **Evenflow** * 3hr Ago   7: LIKE   REPLY
I heard that Nikki's oven is full of bun and that's why Ultragirl was involved.

 **AC** * 12min Ago   0: LIKE   REPLY
Wishful thinking, Yank! Ultragirl stuck her nose where it didn't belong! Worst heel turn ever!

 **Y2Z** * 3hr Ago   0: LIKE   REPLY
When are they going to finally ban piledrivers?

 **Chavez Darwint** * 3hr Ago   10: LIKE   REPLY
I heard that Camille Cote is coming to Rival Angels!

 **Kung Fu Naki** * 2hr Ago   5: LIKE   REPLY
My life would be totes complete.

 **IVORY TOWER** * 4hr Ago   8: LIKE   REPLY
WHEN IS SHANNON GETTING A PUSH?

Y2Z * 2hr Ago   5: LIKE   REPLY
As soon as you take your finger off the CAPS LOCK.

 **Wedgiesock** * 4hr Ago   5: LIKE   REPLY
So...what happens with the TV title now? Is Krystin getting screwed again?

Heated Lime * 4hr Ago   1: LIKE   REPLY
The title is in abeyance.

Wedgiesock * 2hr Ago 5: LIKE   REPLY
What's that mean?

Heated Lime * 2hr Ago 0: LIKE   REPLY
Look it up, dummy. GTFO.

 **MassiveBlokeThChavSlayer** * 5hr Ago   11: LIKE   REPLY
Aphrodite is SO hot.

Season 3
Chapter 1

Art: Alan Evans
Story: Alan Evans and Justin Riley
Color Assists: Aaron Daly
Rival Angels created by Alan Evans
www.RivalAngels.com

BEST DAY EVER!
I'M VERY PROUD OF YOU, SABRINA.
WHATEVER.
NOW.
HOW DO I LOOK?
YOU HAVE NEVER BEEN MORE BEAUTIFUL.
YOU LOOK LIKE A ROCK STAR.
IT'S LIKE WHAT YOU NORMALLY WEAR, BUT WITH DIFFERENT COLORS, SO-.
READY?
LET'S BE BAD GUYS.
READY OR NOT...

"HERE WE COME."
OH MY GOD. THE RUMORS ARE TRUE...
SABRINA MANCINI IS A MEMBER OF DAMAGE INC.!
WHAT?
PFFTTT!
DON'T DO IT, SABRINA!
WHOA.
THE FANS ARE IN SHOCK. WHAT DOES THIS MEAN FOR SABRINA GOING FORWARD?
YAAAYY!!
IT MEANS SHE DOESN'T HAVE TO WORRY ABOUT SORE LOSERS TAKING OUT THEIR FRUSTRATIONS ON HER.
WE'LL HAVE TO SEE IF SABRINA'S NEW DIGS TRANSLATE TO SUCCESS TONIGHT.
ULTRADRAGON HAS A SERIOUS TEST AGAINST TOO HOTT!
NEVER MIND THE NEW LOOK, IT'S THE NEW COMPANY THAT'S IMPORTANT. SUCCESS BREEDS SUCCESS.
PSSSH.
SARA AND LORETTA WOULD LIKE NOTHING BETTER THAN TO SPOIL SABRINA'S COMING OUT PARTY!

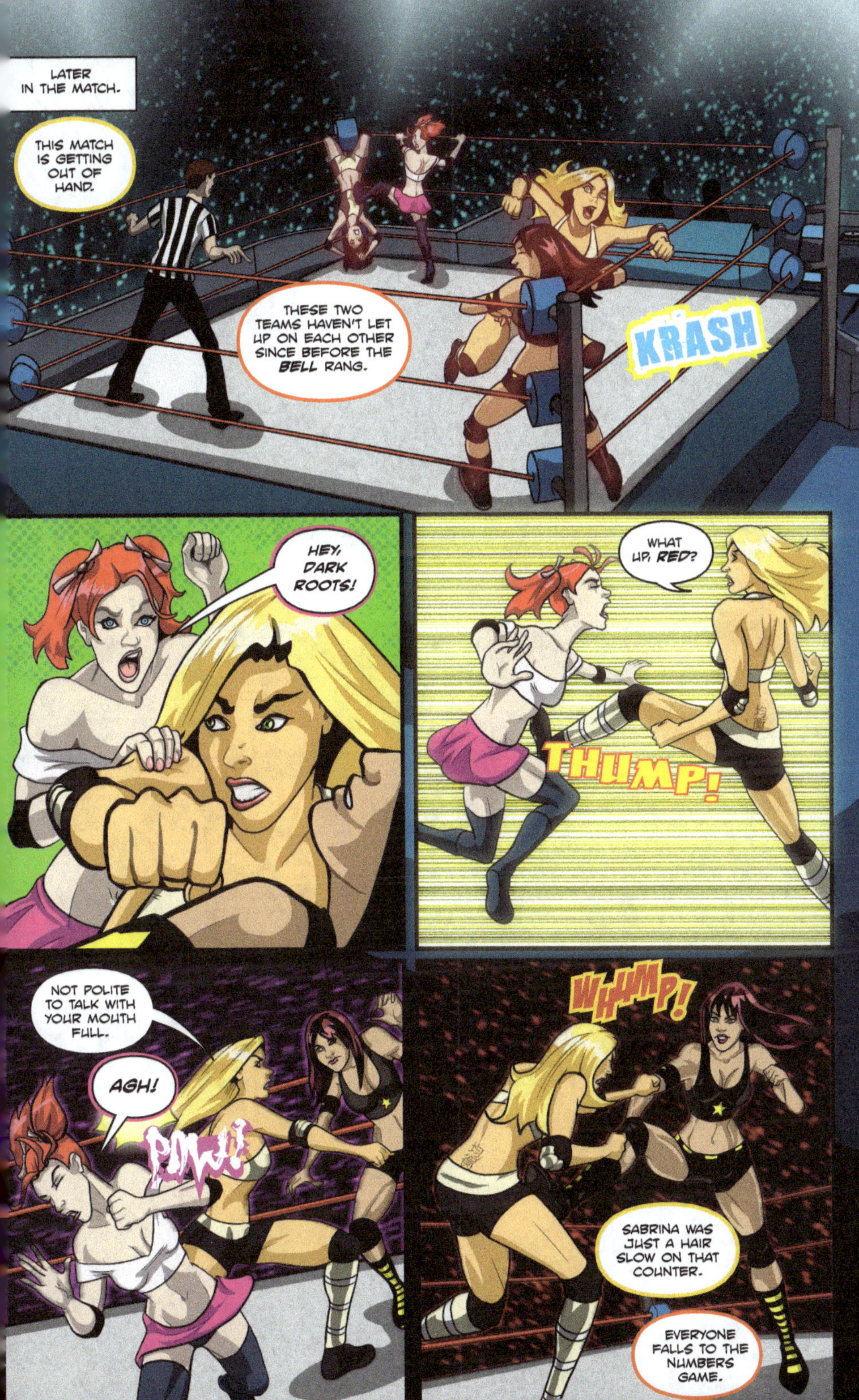

LATER IN THE MATCH.
THIS MATCH IS GETTING OUT OF HAND.
THESE TWO TEAMS HAVEN'T LET UP ON EACH OTHER SINCE BEFORE THE BELL RANG.
KRASH
HEY, DARK ROOTS!
WHAT UP, RED?
THUMP!
NOT POLITE TO TALK WITH YOUR MOUTH FULL.
AGH!
PAW!
WHUMP!
SABRINA WAS JUST A HAIR SLOW ON THAT COUNTER.
EVERYONE FALLS TO THE NUMBERS GAME.

SABRINA'S IN FOR A ROUGH RIDE!
PEDIGREE!
KRASH
GROAN!
THAT'S GOTTA BE IT.
SA-BRI-NA!
SA-BRI-NA!
SA-BRI-NA!
HURRY. THIS BITCH WON'T STAY DOWN FOREVER.
THEY SHOULD GO FOR THE PINFALL.
TOO HOTT KNOWS WHAT THEY'RE DOING.
AFTER SCHOOL SPECIAL!
THERE'S NO CALL FOR THAT. THEY'RE JUST RUNNING UP THE SCORE NOW.
BAM!
WHAT'S THE POINT OF WINNING IF YOU CAN'T WIN BIG?
WINNING JUSTIFIES EVERYTHING!
1....
2...

NINJA'D!
WHERE DID SHE COME FROM?
THAT SNEAKY 'LIL DRAGON' MADE THE SAVE!
BRINA, GET UP!
KRAK!
THUMP!
THIS IS JUST LIKE A MICHAEL BAY MOVIE.
IT'S A TOTAL WRECK!
UL-TRA-DRA-GON!
UL-TRA-DRA-GON!
TOO-HOT!!
TOO-HOT!!
YOUR SIDEKICK'S LITTLE STUNT MEANS I'M KEEPING YOU AFTER SCHOOL.
I THINK SABRINA'S SMILE IS GOING TO BE 'INCOMPLETE' AFTER THAT HARD SHOT.
KRAK!

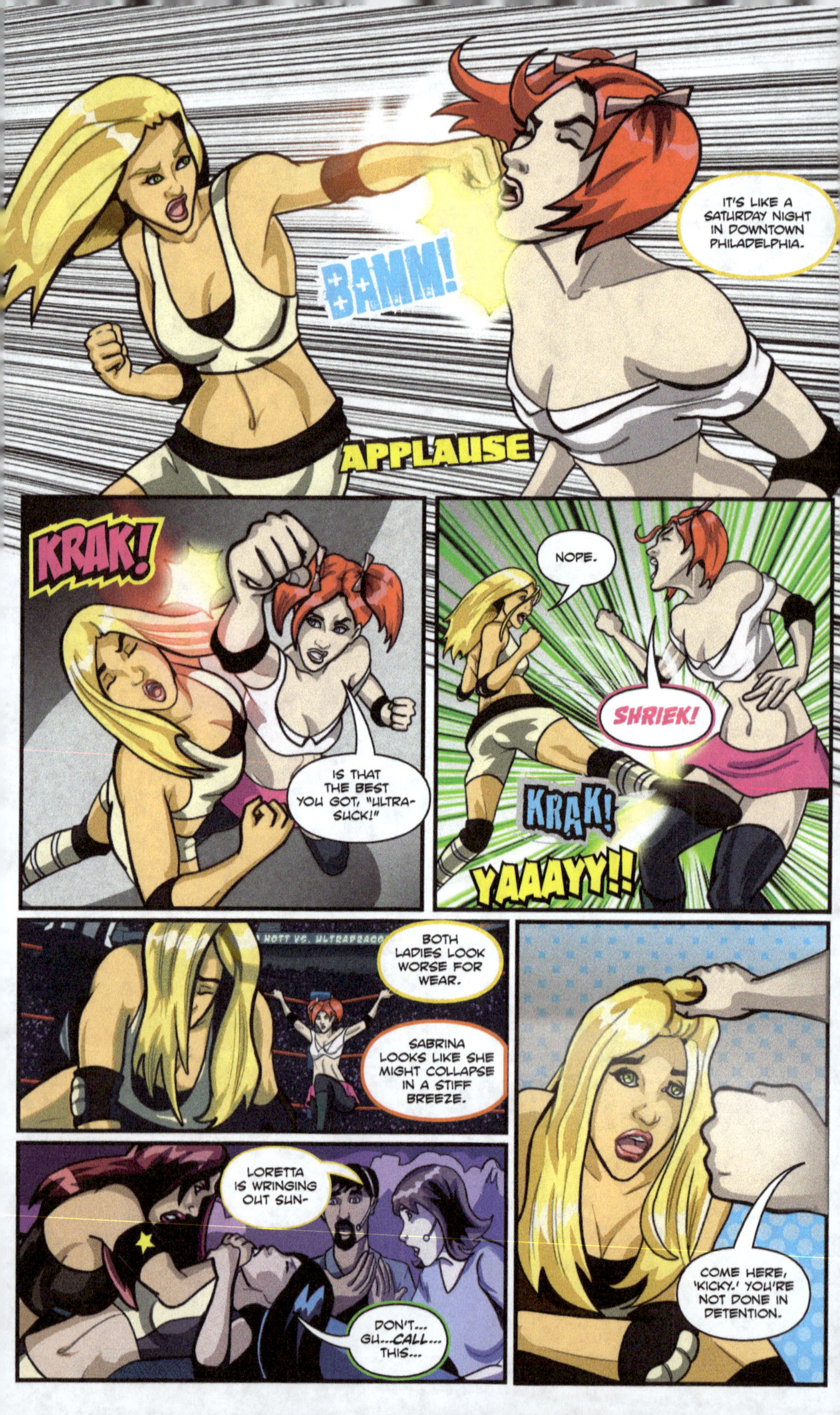

BAMM!
APPLAUSE
IT'S LIKE A SATURDAY NIGHT IN DOWNTOWN PHILADELPHIA.
KRAK!
IS THAT THE BEST YOU GOT, "ULTRA-SUCK!"
NOPE.
SHRIEK!
KRAK!
YAAAYY!!
BOTH LADIES LOOK WORSE FOR WEAR.
SABRINA LOOKS LIKE SHE MIGHT COLLAPSE IN A STIFF BREEZE.
HOTT VS. ULTRADRAGO
LORETTA IS WRINGING OUT SUN-
DON'T... GU...CALL... THIS...
COME HERE, 'KICKY.' YOU'RE NOT DONE IN DETENTION.

YAGH!
OH, SABRINA WASN'T AS HURT AS SHE WAS LETTING ON.
I WOULDN'T BET ON THAT. NO ONE IS THAT GOOD OF AN ACTOR.

MICHINOKU DRIVER!
DEVASTATING COUNTER!
TWUNK
1....
2....
PPFFFFFTTTTTT!
3

LOOKS LIKE SABRINA'S DECISION TO JOIN DAMAGE INC. IS PAYING DIVIDENDS.
DING DING
YAAAYY!!
ULTRADRAGON WAS FORMIDABLE BEFORE. THERE'S NO TELLING WHAT THIS ALLIANCE WILL BRING NOW.

GOOD WIN, LADIES.
SOLID.

EASY NOW. I DIDN'T COME HERE TO FIGHT.
I CAME HERE TO APOLOGIZE.

APOLOGIZE FOR WHAT?
INTERRUPTING OUR VICTORY CELEBRATION?
SOMETHING WE WORKED OUR ASSES OFF FOR?

GET THE XXXX OUT OF HERE, USED-TO-BE-CHAMP!
IT'S OKAY, SUN.

SPEAK YOUR PIECE.

I WANTED TO APOLOGIZE FOR PUTTING YOU THROUGH A TABLE.
I WAS SO INCREDIBLY PISSED AT WHAT YVONNE PULLED AND MY EMOTIONS GOT THE BETTER OF ME.

AND I'M DOUBLY SORRY IF MY ACTIONS MADE THIS HAPPEN.

DON'T FLATTER YOURSELF, CHAM-. BRENDA.
EVERYONE'S BEEN TELLING ME FOREVER TO HAVE SOMEONE WATCH MY BACK.
MY TRIP THROUGH THE TABLE WAS A TESTAMENT TO THAT, SO THANKS.
LIKE BUD FOX SAYING, 'THANKS FOR THE BUSINESS LESSON, MR. GEKKO.'
I'D BE LYING IF THE 13-YEAR-OLD GIRL IN ME DIDN'T MARK OUT A LITTLE BIT THAT BRENDA RUA PUT ME THROUGH A TABLE.
SO, SURE. EVERYTHING'S FORGIVEN.
EVEN IF EVERYTHING ISN'T FORGOTTEN.
CIAO!
HUH.

BACKSTAGE.
WHAT THE HELL WAS THAT?
WHAT WAS WHAT?
I THOUGHT WE WERE GOING TO BEAT THE CRAP OUTTA HER!
WHAT? WHY?
DUH!
OH, THAT.
IF I WANTED TO LAY HER OUT, I WOULD'VE WENT ALL, 'IMPERATOR FURIOSA!' ON HER.
WHY DIDN'T YOU? ARE YOU TIRED?
BECAUSE WHAT I DID WAS CLASSY, WITH A LITTLE BIT OF BITCHY THROWN IN.
THEN, I LEFT HER IN THE RING. IT WAS A CLASSIC ZING.
Damage Incorporated
IT WAS A SHITTY ZING, BRINA.
YOU SHOULD'VE PUT HER THROUGH A TABLE.
THE SOUND A BREAKING TABLE MAKES IS LITERALLY, "ZING!"
OKAY, OKAY, NEXT TIME I'LL PUT HER THROUGH A TABLE.
AND YOU CAN LEG DROP HER FOR EMPHASIS, OR SOMETHING.
Damage Incorporated
YOU BETTER.
AND I WILL.
Dam Incorp

SEE? MANCINI CAN'T KEEP UP WITH US. SHE DOESN'T HAVE THE RIGHT ATTITUDE TO PLAY WITH THE BIG GIRLS.
OF COURSE, SHE DOES! SHE CAN BE A TOTAL BITCH!
HEY!
SORRY, I MEANT, bitchy.
THAT'S NOT BETTER.
YOU'RE DOING IT RIGHT NOW.
DO YOU WANT A HUG?
NO.
WE JUST HAVE TO WORK ON HER RUTH-LESSNESS.
I'LL F**K YOU UP, SUNSHINE.
SEE? HALFWAY THERE.
GREAT MATCH, LADIES.
YOU HANDLED YOURSELF WELL, SABRINA, EVEN AFTER THE SORE LOSER TRIED TO CO-OPT YOUR VICTORY.
WHAT DID I SAY?
I'LL PUT HER THROUGH A TABLE NEXT TIME, YEESH.
BETTER YOU THAN ME.

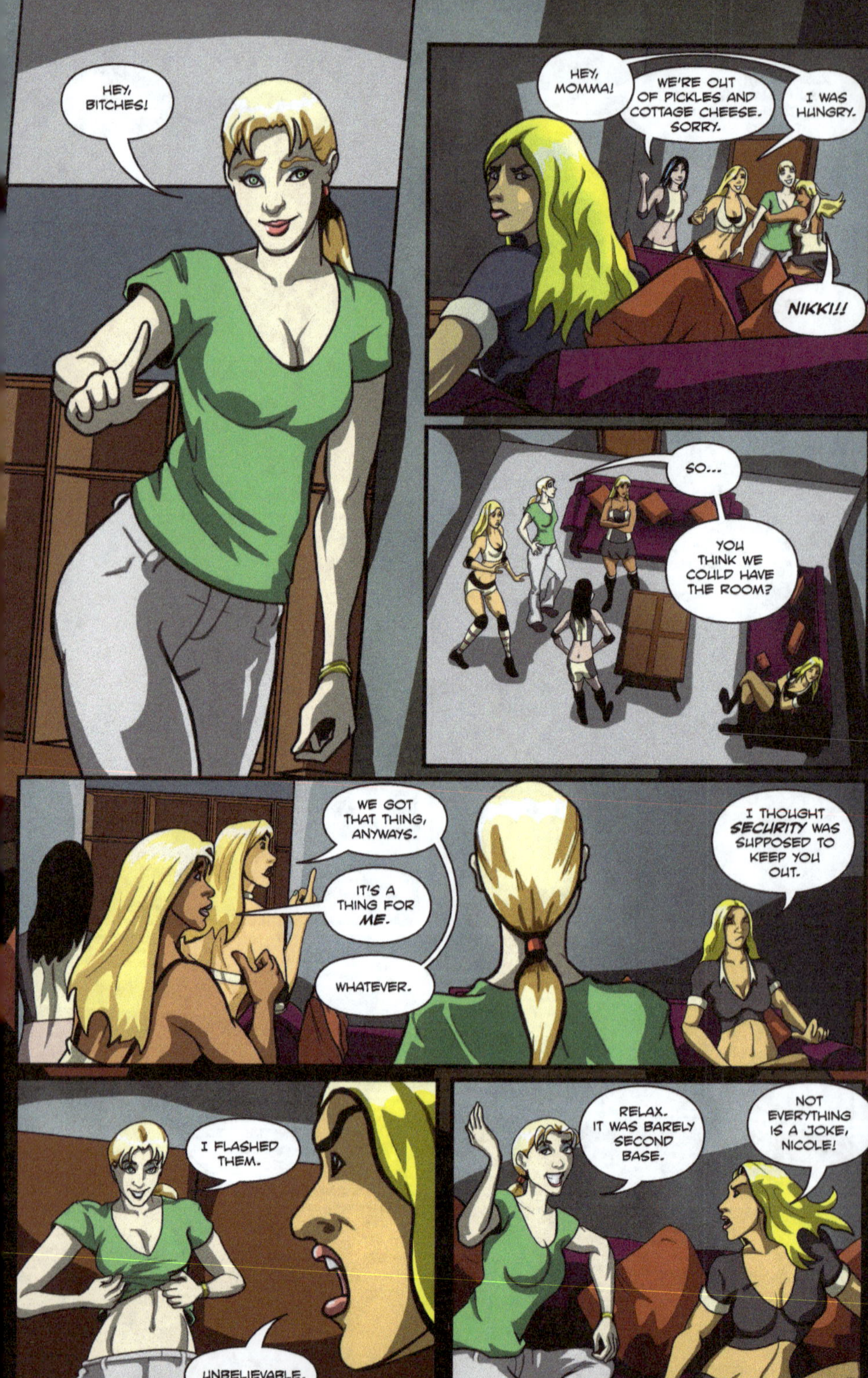

HEY, BITCHES!
HEY, MOMMA!
WE'RE OUT OF PICKLES AND COTTAGE CHEESE. SORRY.
I WAS HUNGRY.
NIKKI!!!
SO...
YOU THINK WE COULD HAVE THE ROOM?
WE GOT THAT THING, ANYWAYS.
IT'S A THING FOR ME.
WHATEVER.
I THOUGHT SECURITY WAS SUPPOSED TO KEEP YOU OUT.
I FLASHED THEM.
UNBELIEVABLE.
RELAX. IT WAS BARELY SECOND BASE.
NOT EVERYTHING IS A JOKE, NICOLE!

WHEN DID YOU FIRST SUSPECT? WERE YOU TRYING TO GET PREGNANT?

OF COURSE, WE WEREN'T TRYING. IT JUST HAPPENED.
'JUST HAPPENED.'
I HAD SUSPICIONS JUST BEFORE I BAILED OUT OF THE TV TITLE MATCH.

THAT LONG? WHY DIDN'T YOU TELL ME?
I KNEW YOU WERE GOING TO WIN BACK THE BELT. I DIDN'T WANT TO OVERSHADOW YOUR SPECIAL DAY.

YOU SILLY GIRL.
YOU'RE HAVING A BABY.
NOTHING COULD OVER-SHADOW THAT.

HAVE I TAUGHT YOU NOTHING, NICOLE?

YOU'RE RIGHT. I'M SORRY, YVONNE.

WILL YOU BE THE GODMOTHER?

Hitch!
YOU LEARNED A FEW THINGS AFTER ALL.

BEFORE THE BREAK, WE SAW A GREAT TAG TEAM MATCH BETWEEN APHRODITE AND HER PARTNER, THE ONE-WOMAN SAMOAN SWAT TEAM, AMANDA BREAKER, AGAINST PREMIERE CHEER.
AND YOU HAVE TO GIVE IT UP TO PREMIERE CHEER FOR TAKING THIS MATCH ON SUCH SHORT NOTICE, AFTER HELL'S BELLES BAILED OUT AT THE LAST MINUTE.
REPLAY
ANGEL HURT HER ACHILLES TENDON IN A FREAK MOPED ACCIDENT. IT'S ALL ABOUT BALANCE. IT COULD HAPPEN TO ANYONE.
I HIGHLY DOUBT IT.
PREMIERE CHEER MADE IT A LIVELY CONTEST.
THUNK
CHEERLEADER NEVEAH TOOK AMANDA OFF OF HER FEET!
THE GODDESS DELIVERED A DIVINE DOUBLE CLOTHESLINE!
BOOOM
SHE NEEDS HOLSTERS FOR THOSE GUNS! HER ARMS, I MEAN!
IT WAS 'GAME OVER' FOR THE CHEERLEADERS AFTER THAT.
CRUSH!!
SERISETTE HAD NO CHOICE BUT TO TAP OUT!
I HEAR THEY'RE STILL PEELING NEVEAH OUT OF THE TURNBUCKLES LIKE A STICKER.
COMING UP NEXT, WE HAVE OUR MUCH-ANTICIPATED TRIPLE THREAT MATCH FOR THE TELEVISION TITLE!
YAAAYY!!

RIVAL ANGELS
TELEVISION CHAMPION
KRYSTIN MOLINE
VS
XTINA CARPENTER
VS
KAT SMITH

I'M NOT SURE THAT KAT HAS ANY BUSINESS BEING IN THIS MATCH.
SHE'S A TWO-TIME CHAMP! OF COURSE SHE'S INVOLVED.
HELL'S BELLES RUINING THE LAST TV CHAMPIONSHIP MATCH HAD NOTHING TO DO WITH THAT?
I'M SURE I DON'T KNOW WHAT YOU MEAN.
DING DING

HEY! THAT'S NOT FAIR!
YAAAYY!!
THIS IS A TRIPLE-THREAT MATCH, NOT A HANDICAP MATCH!

IT LOOKS LIKE XTINA AND KRYSTIN STILL HAVE HARD FEELINGS ABOUT THE WHOLE THING.
TWUNK
HOLDING A GRUDGE HELPS NOBODY.
YAAAYY!!

IT SEEMS THEY'RE FICKLE TOO.
YOU HAD TO KNOW THEIR ALLIANCE WAS TEMPORARY AT BEST.

THERE'S SOME GREAT MAT WRESTLING GOING ON IN THE RING.
BRAK!

OOOOH! DEF TECH'S STOMACH JUST LOST A POINT TO KAT'S BOOT!
WOULD YOU STOP?
BAMM!

KATASTROPHE!
WE'RE GOING TO NEED A SHOVEL TO DIG KRYSTIN OUT OF THE MAT.
ONCE WE FIND KRYSTIN, WE'LL ANNOUNCE WHEN AND WHERE THE SERVICE WILL BE HELD.
WHAM!!

KRYSTIN MIGHT BE IN FOR A ROUGH RIDE!

KRYSTIN DOESN'T LOOK LIKE SHE KNOWS WHAT DAY IT IS.
SHE NEEDS TO RECOVER, AND QUICK. SHE DOESN'T HAVE TO BE PINNED TO LOSE THIS MATCH.

AGH!
OUCH! ON INSTINCT, KRYSTIN HITS THE FIRST PART OF HER 'DIVA BREAKER!'
KRAK!

CHOKESLAM!
KAT IS CLEANING HOUSE!
LET'S MAKE IT 'THREE TIME' CHAMPION FOR KAT SMITH!
BOOOM

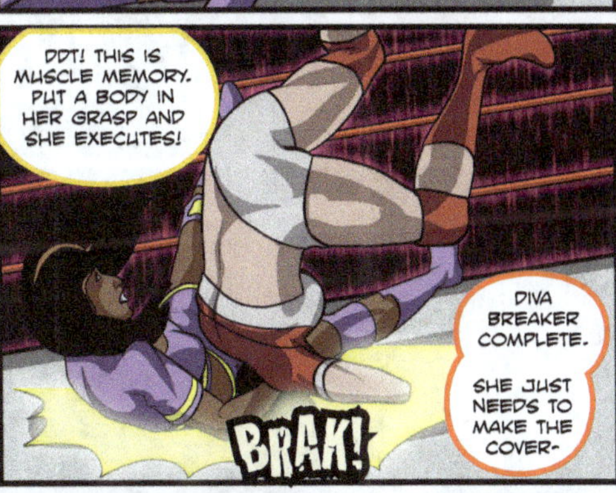

DDT! THIS IS MUSCLE MEMORY. PUT A BODY IN HER GRASP AND SHE EXECUTES!
DIVA BREAKER COMPLETE.
SHE JUST NEEDS TO MAKE THE COVER-
BRAK!

WHAT THE-?
RRGH!
OOOOOOHHHHHHH!
'CANADIAN DYNAMITE' BLEW UP IN DEF TECH'S FACE!
CARPENTER'S GOING TO CAPITALIZE ON KRYSTIN'S OFFENSE!

NOOOOOO!
1...
2...
3

Huff
Huff
HEY, YOU ALMOST HAD IT THERE.
YAAAYY!!

ALMOST.

DON'T YOU WORRY, DEF TECH.
YOU CAN COME BACK TO THE LOCKER ROOM.

ME AND THE GIRLS HAVE A NEW SPOT ALL PICKED OUT FOR YOU.
IT'S THE GARBAGE CAN IN THE CORNER. THE ONE WITH THE LITTLE BASKETBALL HOOP ON IT.

ISN'T THAT GREAT?

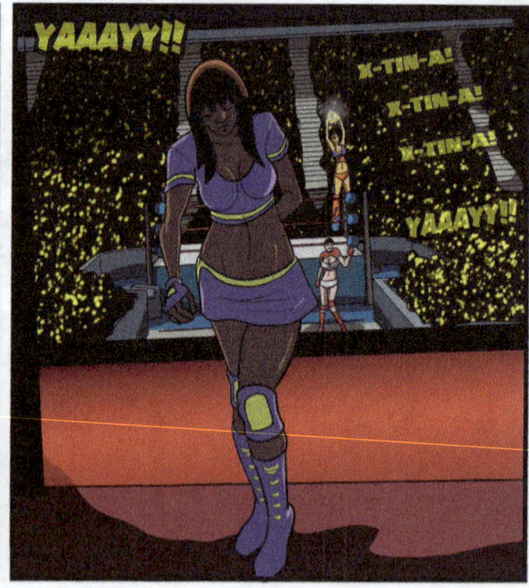

YAAAYY!!
X-TIN-A!
X-TIN-A!
X-TIN-A!
YAAAYY!!

A FEW HOURS LATER.
HA HA HA!
AND THEN HE WAS LIKE...
HA HA HA!
HA HA HA!

"ALLLLLL FOR LOOOOVE!"

HOW ABOUT YVONNE TONIGHT?

I THOUGHT THAT IT WAS OVER FOR HER.
SCRATCH
ARGH!

1....
2....
3
YOU'RE DONE! NO MORE TITLE SHOTS FOR YOU!

BOOOOOO!
CLANG
SHE'S ALWAYS GOT SOMETHING UP HER SLEEVE.

I'M HERE WITH THE WINNER AND STILL WORLD CHAMPION, YVONNE CARMICHAEL AND HER DAMAGE INC. TEAMMATES.
NICHOLAS! THE ANSWER IS, 'YVONNE CARMICHAEL.'
THE QUESTION IS, 'WHO WORE THE WORLD TITLE BETTER?'
CARMICHAEL!
YOU CAN GET A CREAM TO KILL WHATEVER THAT IS ON YOUR FOREHEAD.
YOU GOT A LOT OF NERVE SAYING I WON'T GET A TITLE SHOT AFTER THAT CHEAP STUNT YOU PULLED!
NO WAY THAT STANDS.
WHAT DO YOU PEANUTS THINK YOU'RE DOING?
I THINK ULTRADRAGON STILL HAS SOME HARD FEELINGS TOWARD THE CATGIRLS!
TWUNK
HEH.
SO OUR NEXT MATCH IS AGAINST THE CATGIRLS...

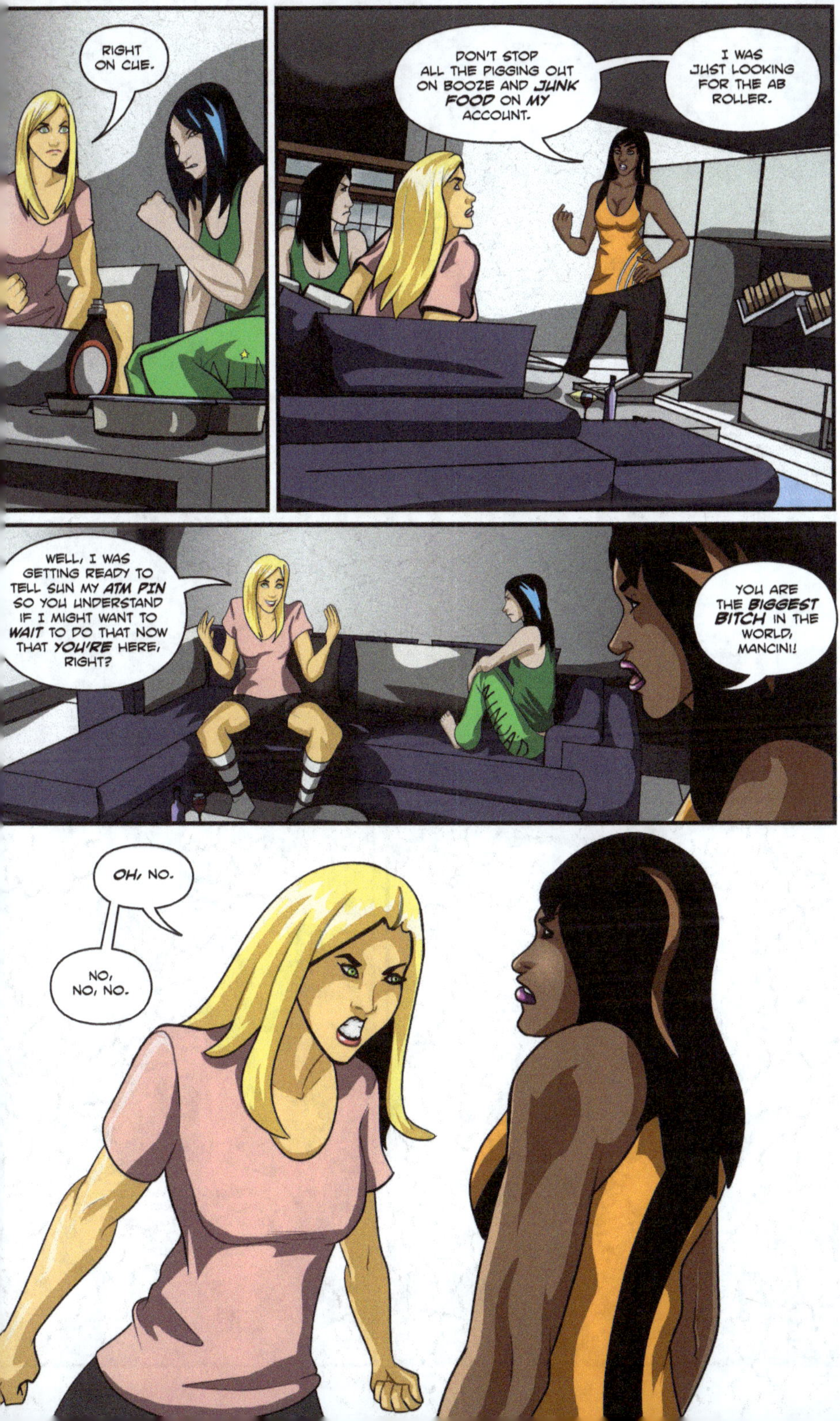

RIGHT ON CUE.

DON'T STOP ALL THE PIGGING OUT ON BOOZE AND JUNK FOOD ON MY ACCOUNT.
I WAS JUST LOOKING FOR THE AB ROLLER.

WELL, I WAS GETTING READY TO TELL SUN MY ATM PIN SO YOU UNDERSTAND IF I MIGHT WANT TO WAIT TO DO THAT NOW THAT YOU'RE HERE, RIGHT?
YOU ARE THE BIGGEST BITCH IN THE WORLD, MANCINI!

OH, NO.
NO, NO, NO.

FIRST, I'D HAVE TO FIND YOUR SUPER DARK SECRET.
THE KIND YOU DON'T WANT ANYONE TO KNOW. THE HUMILIATING KIND.
SECOND, I'D TELL IT IN FRONT OF THE WHOLE WORLD...
...IN FRONT OF YOUR FRIENDS, FAMILY...
MOM...

AND AFTER ALL THAT, THEN I'D BE THE BIGGEST BITCH IN THE WORLD.
UNTIL THEN, I GUESS I'LL HAVE TO SETTLE FOR SECOND PLACE!

YOU DON'T GET IT, MAN!
YOU WERE GONE, TO JAPAN, AND FINALLY...

FINALLY, I HAD A CHANCE TO SHINE ON MY OWN AND NOT AS ONE PIECE OF SOME ROOKIE GIRL GROUP.

AND THEN YOU CAME BACK AND ALL THE ATTENTION WENT BACK TO YOU.
AGAIN.
AND THEN I GOT HURT. BY THOSE F***ING COWARDS!
I KNOW WHAT THAT'S LIKE.
BUT THEN THEY TOOK MY BELT AWAY!
I NEVER LOST IT!
I GOT INTO THE 'IVORY SKYBOX,' AND IT'S REALLY AWESOME THERE.
BUT I'M STILL SEEING YOU, FRONT AND CENTER FROM THAT SKYBOX.
THE CATGIRLS ASKED ME IF I COULD GIVE THEM AN EDGE AGAINST YOU TWO.
THEY WERE REALLY PERSISTENT.
SO THAT'S WHAT YOU TOLD THEM?

TOTALLY NOT MY FINEST MOMENT.

I'D HATE IT IF MY FRIENDS, FAMILY...
MOM FOUND OUT SOMETHING LIKE THAT IN THE WAY THEY FOUND OUT.
SUN, I'M SORR-

FORGET IT!
YOU FEEL GUILTY. CONGRATULATIONS, YOU REALLY ARE HUMAN, BUT YOU'RE STILL HANGING OUT WITH THOSE BITCHES, AREN'T YOU?
WHEN'S YOUR NEXT DEBRIEFING? WILL YOU TELL THEM ABOUT THIS CONVERSATION?

GET OUT OF MY FACE, MANCINI, BEFORE I KNOCK YOUR TEETH OUT.
WOULD THAT BE BEFORE OR AFTER YOU GIVE THE SCOUTING REPORT STRAIGHT FROM MY DIARY ON LIVE TV?
STOP IT YOU GUYS...

AGH!
GET OFF ME, BROOKE!
PASH

O. M. G.
WHATEVER, BROOKE. YOUR RACK'S LIKE A MITHRIL CHAIN SHIRT.

OH, GOD, I THINK YOU RUPTURED IT. IT'S LEAKING...!
WHAT? NO, BROOKE, THAT COULDN'T HAPPEN...

DO I ICE IT... OR PUT HEAT ON IT?
ICE, MAYBE? I DON'T KNOW! SHOULD WE CALL 911?

THANKS, BROOKE.

I KNOW THINGS.

I KNOW YOUR HAND HEALED AT A RIDICULOUSLY ACCELERATED RATE, AND IT WASN'T BECAUSE OF THOSE SMOOTHIES YOU DRINK.

I KNOW OTHER SPORTS DON'T HAVE QUITE THE PESKY RESERVATIONS AND RESTRICTIONS TOWARD DRUGS THAT RIVAL ANGELS DOES.

SAY, MMA FOR INSTANCE.

SOMETHING THAT YOUR BOYFRIEND, TOPHER... SORRY, EX-BOYFRIEND, COULD GET.

EXCEPT, WHAT PHYSICIAN WOULD PRESCRIBE MEDICINE FOR SOMEONE WHO DIDN'T NEED IT?

SOMEONE WITHOUT ANY ETHICS. A REAL SCUMBAG WITH STRANGE IDEAS ABOUT WOMEN IN PAIN NEEDING HIM.

AND WOULDN'T IT FIGURE THAT YOUR EX-BOY-FRIEND IS BFF WITH MY SCUMBAG, SADIST, PIECE OF CRAP EX-BOYFRIEND WHO WAS, OH YEAH, IN SPORTS THERAPY. FOR RIVAL ANGELS.

'WAS' BEING THE KEY WORD THERE.

BECAUSE HE GOT HIS STUPID ASS FIRED, AFTER YOU TOLD SOMEONE ABOUT MY SECRET AND THEY SPILLED IT.

WHAT ARE YOU GOING TO DO?

YOU DON'T HAVE TO WORRY ABOUT ME RATTING YOU OUT.

THAT'S NOT MY STYLE.

BUT IT SEEMS YOU LEFT A LOOSE END DANGLING.

I'M CURIOUS TO SEE IF ANDRE SPILLS ON YOU, OR IF SOMEONE ELSE LOOKS HARD AT WHAT HE'S BEEN DOING THESE PAST FEW MONTHS.

SURE, KRYSTIN.

ALL'S FORGIVEN, EVEN IF IT'S NOT FORGOTTEN.

IT...WILL... TOTALLY FEEL BETTER, IF YOU...
MASSAGE IT.

MAYBE EVEN KISS IT-

AH!
YOU WHORE!
JABI

HAHAHAHA!
SHUT UP, IT AIN'T FUNNY.
OUT OF MY SIGHT FOR A MINUTE AND YOU'RE ALREADY FEELING BROOKE UP, HUH?

SHE TOTALLY WAS. HER HANDS ARE SO GENTLE.
WEIRDLY, I KNOW THAT TO BE TRUE.
SHUT UP, BITCHES!

HA HA HA!
HA HA HA!
HA HA HA!

HA HA HA!
HA HA HA!
HA HA HA

QUADSTAR ★★ GYM ★★
QUADSTAR ★★ GYM ★★

Q4
19:31
Cancel
Camille
Send
To: YCgold@gmail.com
Cc/Bcc, From: Mmacdonald@att.net
Subject: Camille
Training video:
09004.mp4
500.5 MB

MARCEAU!

NETTOYEZ CE GÂCHIS.
END CHAPTER 1

RIVAL ANGELS
CHAPTER 2
"We can not solve our problems with the same level of thinking that created them"
— Albert Einstein

chapter 2
WELCOME BACK EVERYONE.
THE NEXT QUESTION FOR OUR GUESTS...
WHAT ARE YOUR GOALS IN RIVAL ANGELS?
RIVAL ANGELS UNCOVERED
I'M GOING TO CONQUER WRESTLING, OH YES, BUT ALSO MOVIES, MAGAZINES AND RED CARPET EVENTS.
I'M GOING TO BE THE ROCK AND TAYLOR SWIFT ALL ROLLED UP INTO ONE.
I WANT TO BE THE BIGGEST POP CULTURE ICON THE WORLD HAS EVER SEEN. MY FACE EVERYWHERE. WHO WOULDN'T WANT TO SEE THAT?
I WILL BE THE MOST DOMINANT ATHLETE EVER.
PERIOD.
I'M GOING TO COLLECT ALL THE GOLD.
WORLD, TAG TEAM AND TELEVISION CHAMPION.
I'M GOING TO BE THE FIRST EVER...
TRIPLE CROWN CHAMPION.
BOOM.
I'M GOING TO BE THE MOST EXCITING WRESTLER OF ALL TIME.
GET OUT THE RED PEN AND START EDITING THE HISTORY BOOKS!

EXCITING?
EXCITING'S NOT HARD. FLASH THE CROWD AND YOU'RE EXCITING FOR THE REST OF THE NEWS CYCLE.

NOT WHAT I MEAN. I MEAN EXCITING LIKE ELECTRIC ANTICIPATION AND AN OVERFLOW OF EMOTION WHEN MY MUSIC HITS. EYES GLUED TO THE MATCH AND BREATH CATCHING IN THROATS.

EXCITING.

FLIPPY DIPPY'S GOOD FOR A POP ON THE NIGHT OF THE SHOW, AND I'M NOT MAD AT A JAWBREAKING SUPERKICK, BUT GOLD IS THE STANDARD MEASUREMENT OF EXCELLENCE. SO I WANT ALL OF IT, ALL OF THE EXCELLENCE.

I WANT TO BE THE ONE WHO HEADLINES THE CARD WHETHER THERE'S A BELT INVOLVED OR NOT. I WANNA DRAW THE HOUSES AND THE BUYS BECAUSE THE PEOPLE SEE MY NAME AND READ IT AS, "GUARANTEED THE BEST SHOW IN TOWN."

YEAH, YEAH, YEAH.

AS I WAS SAYING, FOR MY FIRST YEAR, I DON'T SEE ANYTHING LESS THAN ROOKIE OF THE YEAR.

SOME PEOPLE MIGHT SAY THAT'S ARROGANT, BUT I SET THE BAR HIGH FOR MYSELF AND I'LL SHOW EVERYONE WHAT I ALREADY KNOW...

THAT I'M THE BEST WRESTLER.

PERIOD.

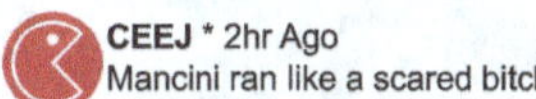 **CEEJ** * 2hr Ago   5: **LIKE**   **REPLY**
Mancini ran like a scared bitch.

 **Evenflow** * 2hr Ago   8: **LIKE**   **REPLY**
Huh? She shook hands and left. Sabrina is a classy lady.

 **Chick Hera** * 1hr Ago 2: **LIKE**   **REPLY**
Left like a bitch! Mancini gets grabbed its all over.

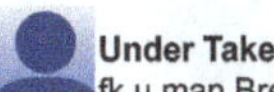 **Under Taker24** * 3hr Ago   1: **LIKE**   **REPLY**
fk u man Bren is the goat also Mancini is stupd Bren wast even tryng first time and Mancini bout 2 git slaped.

 **Evenflow** * 2hr Ago   6: **LIKE**   **REPLY**
Hate to say it but I agree. Rua destroys Mancini like @Under Taker24 here just destroyed the English language.

 **Chavez Darwint** * 2hr Ago   10: **LIKE**   **REPLY**
Bow down to Queen Yvonne! FTW!

 **Mr. Logic** * 2hr Ago   4: **LIKE**   **REPLY**
This defies logic. Yvonne's specialty is eye pokes and did it to retain. Don't bow to that.

 **HEY HOW R U** * 1hr Ago   7: **LIKE**   **REPLY**
It worked, nut hugger. Yvonne's the champ. Deal with it.

 **GEE MAN** * 3hr Ago   5: **LIKE**   **REPLY**
I heard that Camille Cote is coming soon.

 **Zomaya** * 4hr Ago   1: **LIKE**   **REPLY**
SOURCE???

 **Under Taker24** * 2hr Ago   5: **LIKE**   **REPLY**
Ur mom

 **IVORY TOWER** * 3hr Ago   0: **LIKE**   **REPLY**
WHEN IS SHANNON GETTING HER TITLE SHOT?

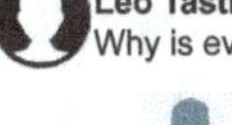 **AC** * 3hr Ago   10: **LIKE**   **REPLY**
Doesn't matter. She'll lose because she's mid-card and Irish.

 **Leo Tastic** * 4hr Ago   5: **LIKE**   **REPLY**
Why is everyone hating on Krystin? She got robbed of her belt, never pinned.

  **Kung Fu Naki** * 4hr Ago   4: **LIKE**   **REPLY**
Its what happens when you treat people like shit.

 **Chick Hera** * 2hr Ago 2: **LIKE**   **REPLY**
Everyone hates her. Who cares.

 **Wedgiesock** * 4hr Ago   11: **LIKE**   **REPLY**
I totes need some DD goDDess

  **Heated Lime** * 4hr Ago   1: **LIKE**   **REPLY**
Hell's Belles needz to stop running from her.

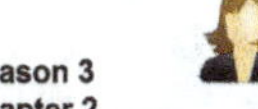 **Tricep Meat** * 2hr Ago 3: **LIKE**
Has super tits don't win matches.

Kat's Tears * 2hr Ago 8: **LIKE**
Is simple discussion too much to ask?

Season 3
Chapter 2

Art: Alan Evans
Story: Alan Evans and Justin Riley
Color Assists: Aaron Daly
Rival Angels created by Alan Evans
www.RivalAngels.com

MORNING.
SINKERS SUCK.

Topher
Message

PLEASE STOP TEXTING ME.

MONDAY NIGHT.
RIVAL ANGELS

KRYSTIN?
ARE YOU CHANGING... OUT HERE?
SHHHHHH!

WHY AREN'T YOU IN THE 'IVORY,' ER, I MEAN, THE SKYBOX LOCKER ROOM?

I DON'T KNOW.

BUT IT DOESN'T FEEL RIGHT.
AND I NEED TO FEEL RIGHT AGAIN IF I'M GOING TO GET MY BELT BACK.

COME ON.
WHERE ARE WE GOING?

THE HALLWAYS ARE NOWHERE FOR A TALENT LIKE YOU.

YOU'RE COMING BACK TO THE LOCKER ROOM.
TAKE THE ONE NEXT TO AMANDA AND ME.
I DON'T KNOW.

THANKS, BROOKE.
WELL, YOU HAVE BEEN SEEN WITH ME. THIS IS NO TIME TO BACKSLIDE.

OH!
GOOD LUCK IN YOUR MATCH TONIGHT, LADIES!

WOW. WHATEVER.
GIVE IT SOME TIME. THEY'LL COME AROUND.

I DON'T KNOW IF THIS WAS SUCH A GOOD IDEA.
WHY?
IT'S TRUE THAT THERE'S SOME SHADE BEING THROWN AROUND, BUT IT'S NOT ALL DIRECTED AT YOU. HANDLING JEALOUSY IS THE TRUE TEST OF A SUPERSTAR.
DON'T LET THE HATERS GET TO YOU.
YOU'RE ABSOLUTELY RIGHT, AMANDA.
AND YOU KNOW WHAT?
HOW ABOUT I COME DOWN FOR YOUR TAG MATCH TONIGHT AGAINST HELL'S BELLES TONIGHT? TO CHECK THEIR DUPLICITOUS WAYS?
SURE.
WHY NOT?

YAAAAAYYY!!
TORQUE IT!
QUIT HOLDING HER WRIST LIKE SHE'S YOUR DATE!
NOT LIKE THAT, AMANDA! LIKE THIS! RIGHT?
COME ON! YOU WANT TO WIN, RIGHT?
BOOOOOO!
IT'S ALL OVER, SILICONE AND HALITOSIS.
OH HELL.

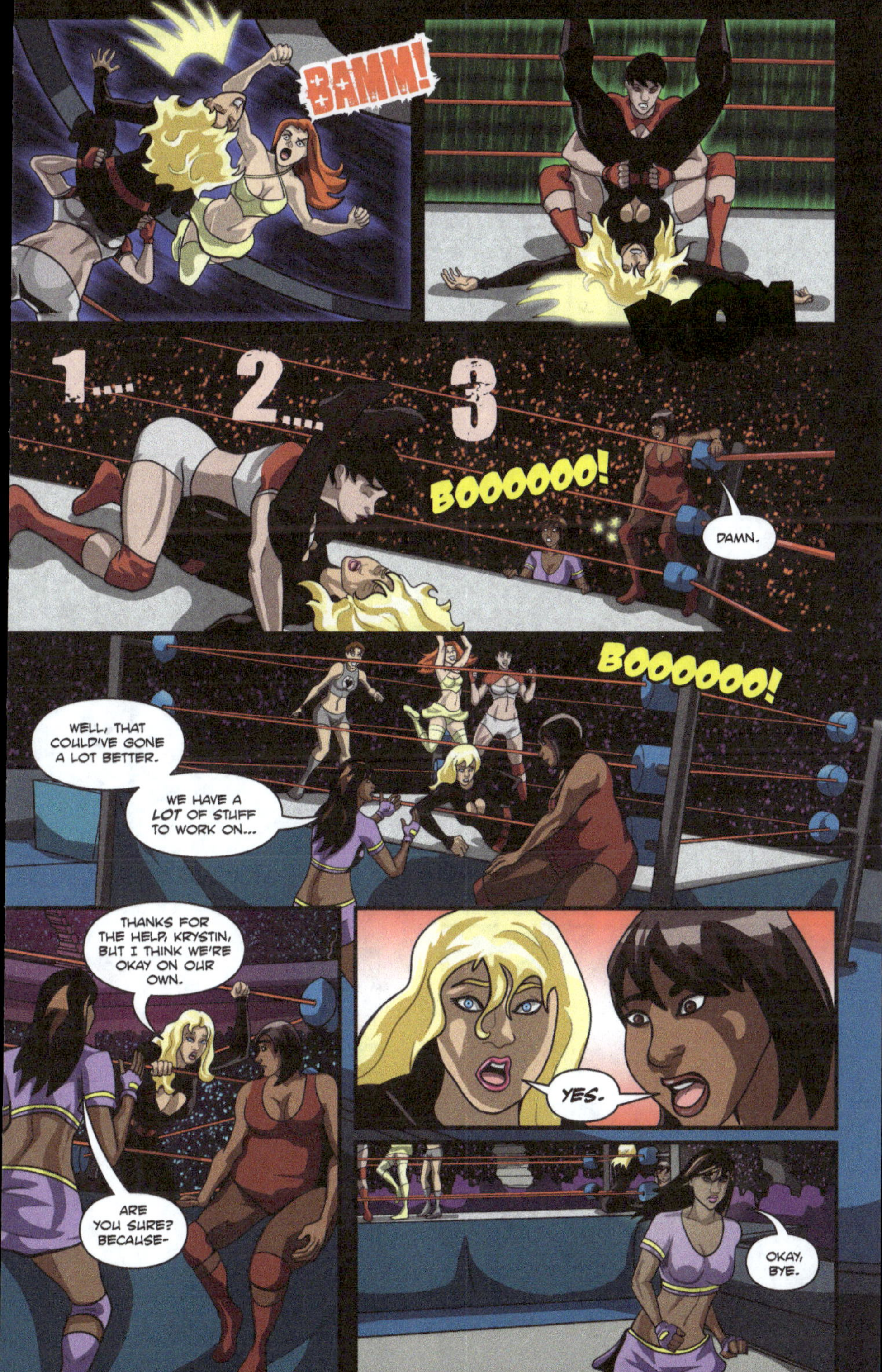

BAMM!
1....
2....
3
BOOOOOO!
DAMN.
BOOOOOO!
WELL, THAT COULD'VE GONE A LOT BETTER.
WE HAVE A LOT OF STUFF TO WORK ON...
THANKS FOR THE HELP, KRYSTIN, BUT I THINK WE'RE OKAY ON OUR OWN.
YES.
ARE YOU SURE? BECAUSE-
OKAY, BYE.

THAT WAS BULL AND YOU KNOW IT!

YVONNE CHEATED!
BRENDA, YOU'VE ALREADY HAD YOUR REMATCH.
SHANNON MCCOURT HAS THE NEXT TITLE SHOT WITH YVONNE.

I CAN'T PLAN PAST THAT RIGHT NOW.

WHAT ABOUT CAMILLE COTE?
WHAT ABOUT HER?

IS SHE GETTING A TITLE SHOT?
IT'S...IT'S COMPLICATED.

PATHETIC EXCUSES USUALLY ARE.

WE HAVE TWO GREAT WRESTLERS MAKING THEIR DEBUT TONIGHT, JEFF.
THAT'S RIGHT DAWN. WE HAVE KIM HART AGAINST THE OLYMPIC MEDALIST, CAMILLE COTE!
YAAAYY!!
DING DING
BRAK!
CAMILLE DOESN'T WASTE ANY TIME IN GOING AFTER KIM!
OLYMPIANS DON'T NEED TO WARM UP. THEY'RE ALREADY HOT!
I HOPE KIM HAS A GOOD CHIROPRACTOR ON SPEED DIAL.
THUNK
CALF SLICER!
AAAAAHHHHHH!
TAP!! TAP!! TAP!!
THE FRENCH CANADIAN BROUGHT HER A-GAME TONIGHT.
WHAT A WICKED SUBMISSION!
C'EST FAIT.
CAMILLE'S DEBUT MATCH IS MAJORLY SUCCESSFUL.
WHAT A SPECTACULAR FIRST IMPRESSION.

BACKSTAGE.
PROFESSOR SHANNON MCCOURT, NOW THAT YOU'RE THE #1 CONTENDER FOR THE RIVAL ANGELS WORLD CHAMPIONSHIP,
WHEN DO YOU THINK YOU'LL CHALLENGE YVONNE FOR THE TITLE?
WELL, NICK, I'VE BEEN TRAINING ALL OF MY LIFE FOR THIS MOMENT-
HOLD IT!
BRENDA RUA? WHAT ARE-
HUH?
SHANNON, I'M HERE TO CHALLENGE YOU FOR YOUR #1 CONTENDER'S SPOT.
THE FANS HAVE BEEN WANTING FOR US TO COMPETE AGAINST EACH OTHER.
THE PRIZE WILL BE MORE THAN ENOUGH INCENTIVE TO BRING OUT THE BEST IN US.
IT WILL BE A GREAT MATCH.
THANKS BUT NO THANKS, BRENDA. RESPECTFULLY.
I HAVE MY FOCUS SET ON WINNING THE WORLD TITLE.
MAYBE SOME OTHER TIME-
IT'S A GOOD THING THAT DECISION ISN'T UP TO YOU.
WAIT, WHAT? WHAT ARE YOU TALKING ABOUT?
SOMETHING TELLS ME WE'RE GOING TO SEE THAT #1 CONTENDER'S MATCH AFTER ALL.

WHAT IS SHE PLAYING AT?
SHOULD WE BOOK BRENDA VS. SHANNON FOR THE #1 CONTENDER'S SPOT FOR NEXT WEEK?

GABRIELLE!
WE NEED TO TALK.
I SUPPOSE YOU WANT ANOTHER SHOT AT THE TV TITLE?

I WANT A MATCH WITH ROSE.
RIGHT NOW.
WHAT?!

I THOUGHT WE WERE FRIENDS.
SHUT YOUR MOUTH. IT'S DONE ENOUGH DAMAGE.
WE HAVE A TAG MATCH WITH ULTRADRAGON TONIGHT.

I NEED THIS GABRIELLE.
I'LL CASH IN ALL MY FAVORS TO GET THIS.

HAHAHA-HAHA!
'FAVORS.' PLURAL.

I.... UH...
NO PROBLEM. YOU GOT YOUR MATCH WITH ROSE.

WHAT?!
THANK YOU, GABRIELLE. I OWE YOU.
I KNOW.

WHAT ABOUT THE TAG MATCH WITH ULTRADRAGON?
IT'S STILL ON, OF COURSE. THE FANS ARE DYING TO SEE THEM GET THEIR HANDS ON YOU.

SO YOU WANT ROSE TO FIGHT TWICE IN ONE NIGHT?

RELAX.
EVERYTHING IS UNDER CONTROL.
BOOK KRYSTIN VS ROSE FOR TONIGHT, MICHAEL.

SHOULD WE BOOK THE MATCH BETWEEN BRENDA AND SHANNON TOO?
ONLY IF SHE HOLDS UP HER END OF THE BARGAIN.

WELL THIS MATCH CAME OUT OF NOWHERE, DAWN.
MYSTERIOUS TOO, SINCE THE CATGIRLS ARE SCHEDULED TO FIGHT ULTRADRAGAON LATER THIS EVENING.
MAYBE ROSE LOST A BET? HA HA!

ROSE LOOKS CONCERNED.
YOU WOULD TOO IF YOU WERE PULLING DOUBLE DUTY.

DING DING
THUD!
KRYSTIN CERTAINLY ISN'T WASTING TIME.
IT'S NOT LIKE SHE GETS PAID BY THE HOUR.
KRYSTIN IS JUST RELENTLESS IN HER ATTACK.
KRAK!

I'M NOT SURE WHAT'S WITH THE AGGRESSION, BUT I LIKE IT.
WHAM!!
I'VE HEARD RUMBLINGS ABOUT SOME LOCKER ROOM TENSION FOLLOWING KRYSTIN AROUND. MAYBE THIS IS A MESSAGE TO HER DETRACTORS.
BRING IT BACK IN, KRYSTIN!
DEF TECH JUST KICKED ROSE'S FACE OFF! SHE SKINNED A CAT!

YOU CAN'T WIN A MATCH OUTSIDE THE RING!
KRYSTIN KNOWS THAT. SHE'S OBVIOUSLY MAKING A POINT. OR A STATEMENT. OR—
AGH!

BACK IN THE RING, MOLINE. I MEAN IT!
BACK IN THE RING, HUH?
UHNFF!

AGGGHH!
NOT WHAT I MEANT, AND YOU KNOW IT.
BREAK THE HOLD!
1...
2...
3...
4...

SORRY, ROSE. THIS ISN'T OVERLY PERSONAL.
YANK!

BLOCK
FUNNY. FEELS PERSONAL.

NOPE.
AGGGHHH! GAH! STOP!
KRAK!
KRAK!
SOMEDAY YOU MIGHT UNDERSTAND.
ANYONE WOULD AFTER THAT BRUTAL OFFENSE.
THIS WAS NEVER ABOUT WINNING OR LOSING.
WHAT IS SHE DOING? WIN THE MATCH, DEF TECH!
ROSE IS FADING FAST.
ROSE IS GOING TO TAP OUT!
LOOKS LIKE ROSE WILL WIN BY COUNTOUT.
THAT'S A DAMN SHAME.
THERE'S OBVIOUSLY MORE TO THIS STORY THAN IT SEEMS AND ONLY THE PARTIES INVOLVED WILL EVER KNOW.
YOU'D HAVE TO BE DENSE NOT TO THINK THIS HAS SOMETHING TO DO WITH THE CATGIRLS MATCH AGAINST ULTRADRAGON.
MAYBE THIS HAS SOMETHING TO DO WITH OUTING SUN'S-
TIME FOR A COMMERCIAL BREAK, JEFF!

YEAH!
DID YOU SEE THAT? THAT WAS GREAT.
YEAH, WHAT WAS THAT ABOUT?
DON'T YOU GET IT?
WE'RE EVEN!
HUH?

I TOOK ROSE OUT AND NOW SUN AND SABRINA WILL GET THEIR WIN AND A SHOT AT THE TAG TEAM TITLES.
AND THEN EVERYTHING WILL BE BACK TO NORMAL AGAIN.
GENIUS, RIGHT?
YOU STUPID BITCH. YOU JUST DON'T LEARN.
YOU JUST SCREWED SUN AND SABRINA.

YAAAAAYYY!!
NEXT WE HAVE A BIG RETURN MATCH, CATGIRLS VS ULTRADRAGON.
CHECK THAT, DAWN, GRUDGE MATCH.
BUT HOW COMPETITIVE OF A MATCH IS IT GOING TO BE AFTER THE MUGGING THAT ROSE TOOK EARLIER?
SNOWKITTEN IS ONE OF THE BEST TAG TEAM SPECIALISTS, BUT IT'S ASKING TOO MUCH FOR HER TO TAKE ON ULTRADRAGON, EFFECTIVELY, BY HERSELF.
HERE SHE COMES! LOOK AT THE DETERMINATION ON HER FACE.
SHE SHOULD DO THE SMART THING AND JUST SIT THIS ONE OUT.
GRAB A CHAIR AND SIT. OR HIT SOMEONE WITH IT. SURE, YOU WON'T WIN THE MATCH, BUT AT LEAST YOU WON'T GET ROSE'D.
YAAAYY!!
ULTRADRAGON DOESN'T SEEM TO MIND THE ODDS IN THEIR FAVOR.
WHY SHOULD THEY? DID THEY AIR SOMEONE'S SECRET ON TV?
IT LOOKS LIKE SNOWKITTEN HAS A SURPRISE FOR US.
I HATE SURPRISES.
RIVAL ANGELS
YAAAYY!!
OH MY GOD.
THAT MUSIC CAN ONLY MEAN ONE THING...

YAAAAAYYY!
IT'S BRENDA RUA!
IS SHE SNOWKITTEN'S PARTNER TONIGHT?
SHE SHOWS UP TO HELP HER BUDDY, AFTER SHE DEMANDS A #1 CONTENDER'S MATCH WITH SHANNON?
NOT SURE HOW MUCH OF A SURPRISE THIS IS.
YOU'RE SO CYNICAL, JEFF. THIS IS GOING TO BE A CLASSIC.
IT SEEMS LIKE SNOWKITTEN WON'T HAVE TO GO THIS MATCH ALONE.
NO SLIGHT TO ROSE, BUT BRENDA'S AN UPGRADE.
SABRINA LOOKS LIKE SOMEONE SPOILED 'STAR WARS' FOR HER.
COME ON!
SABRINA SEEMS RILED UP.
THAT'S WHAT HAPPENS WHEN YOU PUT SOMEONE THROUGH A TABLE.
THEY GET RILED UP.
SABRINA!
THEY MOVED PAST THAT.
HA! DAWN, YOU'RE HILARIOUS!

UL-TRA-DRA-GON!
UL-TRA-DRA-GON!
UL-TRA-DRA-GON!
I WANT TO START!
SETTLE DOWN, YOU MANIAC.
LOOK, SUN, WE—
SHUT UP.
I TRIED.
NO.
BELIEVE IT OR NOT, ALL YOU'VE DONE IS PISS BOTH OF US OFF EVEN MORE.
WE'VE ALL HAD CRUMMY EXES. GET OVER IT.
YOU BET. I'LL GET STARTED ON THAT ONCE I FREE MY FOOT FROM UP IN YOUR PUNK ASS.
DING DING

TWIST!
REVERSE!
SWEEP!
HUP!
FLOAT OVER
ESCA
WHIFF!
YAH!
GRAB
OOF!
YANK!
SQUEEZE
GAH!
ESCAPE
APPLAUSE
APPLAUSE
APPLAUSE

CRUSH!!
AVALANCHE!
BRENDA AND SNOW HAVE BEEN IN CONTROL FOR MOST OF THIS MATCH.
BRAK!
LIKE A GOOD TAG TEAM, THEY'VE CUT SUN OFF FROM SABRINA.
CHOKE!
SUN HAS EACH AND EVERY COMEBACK CUT SHORT.
WHICH ISN'T SURPRISING SINCE SNOW IS A TAG TEAM SPECIALIST...
AND BRENDA IS THE POUND FOR POUND #1 WRESTLER IN THE WORLD.
YAAAYY!!
WHACK!!!
WHAT A BEAUTIFUL SPINNING PELE KICK!

DRA-GON!
DRA-GON!
THIS IS SUN'S CHANCE! CAN SHE MAKE THE TAG?
DRA-GON!
IT MIGHT BE HER LAST CHANCE!

TAG!
YAAAYY!!

SABRINA'S ABOUT TO EXPLODE!
POW!

AGH!
KRAK!
ULTRAKICK!
GOOD NIGHT, BRENDA!

WHAT ARE YOU-?
THAT'S AN INTERESTING STRATEGY BY SNOWKITTEN.
GRAB

?

HOW IS BRENDA STILL STANDING AFTER SABRINA'S ULTRAKICK?
THAT'S WHAT SABRINA WANTS TO KNOW!

AH, SHI-

WHIFF!
-IT!
HOW DID SABRINA DODGE THAT KICK?
SHE'S LUCKY SHE DID, OR HER HEAD WOULD'VE BEEN FOUND IN THE SKYBOX!
OH HELL, NO.
SHE MIGHT'VE OUTSMARTED HERSELF.
SHE'S GOT NOWHERE TO GO!
BAM!
OH, THAT SNEAKY NINJA!
A TIMELY INTERVENTION BY THE LIL DRAGON!
LOOK OUT BELOW!
THAT'S AN UGLY SPILL TO THE OUTSIDE FOR BOTH LADIES.

SABRINA'S BACK UP ON HER FEET.
BRENDA'S GOT AN IRON CLAD DEFENSE.
BLOCK
THAT KICK WOULD'VE CRACKED CONCRETE.
BLOCK
HOW LONG CAN SABRINA PUSH THIS PACE?
WHAT THE HELL, MANCINI?!
BLOCK
HOLY CRAP, THAT WORKED!
HUH?
THUD!
HA HA HA!
ULTRADRAGON IS SHOWING THAT TAG TEAM UNITY THAT'S PUT THEM IN A POSITION TO CHALLENGE FOR THE TAG TEAM TITLES.
AND THAT THEY'RE MENTAL CASES.
ANOTHER ULTRAKICK!
KRAK!
THAT'S GOTTA BE IT FOR BRENDA, RIGHT?
UHNFF!
YAAAYY!!
THE CROWD IS ALMOST AS FIRED UP AS ULTRADRAGON!
WOOOOOOOO!

HERE COMES SNOWKITTEN TO EVEN THE SCORE!
PPFFFFFTTTTTT!
YAAAAAHHHHHHH!!
SPLATT!
THE GOOD NEWS IS THAT SHE STUCK THE LANDING.
GROAN!
THE THREE COUNT IS ACADEMIC.
THIS IS ULTRADRAGON'S CHANCE TO GRAB VICTORY!
ULTRASPLASH!
NO PIN, SABRINA!
WHAT THE #### ARE YOU TALKING ABOUT?!

SNOW ISN'T THE LEGAL PERSON.
BRENDA IS!

?

OKLAHOMA ROLL!
1....
2....
3

APPLAUSE
WHAT THE HELL WAS THAT?!

THAT'S TWO IN A ROW, BITCHES!
TAKES MORE THAN WEARING GOLD TO BE A CHAMPION!

WOW, WHAT A HEARTBREAKING LOSS.
YEP. BACK TO THE DRAWING BOARD FOR ULTRADRAGON.

HEY, YOU *TRIED*.

I'M SORRY, SUN.

YOU COULDN'T HAVE KNOWN...*THAT* WAS GOING TO HAPPEN.

DON'T WORRY ABOUT IT. WE CAN'T WIN THEM ALL.

WELL, *YEAH* THAT, BUT I MEAN, *ALL* OF IT.
HUH?

THIS WAS *PUNISHMENT* FOR YOU GOING OFF-SCRIPT WHEN GABRIELLE FORCED US TO FIGHT EACH OTHER.
BRINA, WHAT THE *HELL* ARE YOU TALKING ABOUT?

I'M CALLING IT. I'M GOING TO GET YOU OUT OF THIS.
I'M GOING TO GET US OUT OF THIS.
YOU SHOULD BE FIGHTING FOR TITLES, SINGLES TITLES.
BUT—
YOU'RE MAGNIFICENT. YOU'VE BEEN A CHAMPION.
IT'S MY RESPONSIBILITY. YOU DON'T DESERVE THIS.
SUNSHINE...
ARE WE STILL—
YES.
FOREVER AND—
DUH.

KREEAK

SABRINA?

HEY, BITCH.

TOUGH LOSS. DON'T TELL ULTRA-BRAT I SAID SO.

SHE'S TRENDING THOUGH.

"#CAN'TWIN THEBIGONE."

ISN'T THAT HILARIOUS?

#YOUCAN EATABIGONE.

HOLY CRAP, TAKE IT EASY. BOTH OF YOUR WIN-LOSS RECORDS ARE BETTER THAN MINE.

FANS ARE ASSHOLES WITH ATTENTION SPANS LESS THAN GOLD-FISH.

WAITAMINUTE? WHERE'S SABRINA?

NOOOOOOO.

YOU GUYS BROKE UP?

WHAT DO YOU CARE? YOU HATE SABRINA.

YOU DON'T!

NIKKI SAYS YOU DON'T HAVE TO BE BEST FRIENDS TO BE A GOOD TAG TEAM, BUT ALL THE BEST TEAMS WERE!

THE ROAD WARRIORS! THE STEINERS! FREEBIRDS! MAXWELL AND HAZZARD! BLACK AND BLUE!

YOU TWO ALMOST LOST YOUR JOBS BECAUSE OF YOUR RIDICULOUS LOYALTY!

HMMM. MAYBE YOU GUYS AREN'T THAT GOOD OF FRIENDS...

FINE. HAVE IT YOUR WAY.

IT'S NOT YOUR FAULT, SABRINA.
I DO WANT TO BE A SINGLES CHAMP.
I WANT TO BE THE TELEVISION CHAMPION.
I WANT TO BE THE WORLD CHAMPION.
BUT I'VE ALWAYS WANTED TO BE THE FIRST EVER TRIPLE CROWN CHAMPION, SO I NEED TO WIN THE TAG TITLES.
BEING IN A TAG TEAM WAS UNEXPECTED, BUT NOT UNWANTED.
ESPECIALLY THE PART ABOUT BEING YOUR TAG PARTNER.
I'M NOT ANY CLOSER TO ANY OF THAT THAN WHEN I STARTED.
SIGH.
EXIT

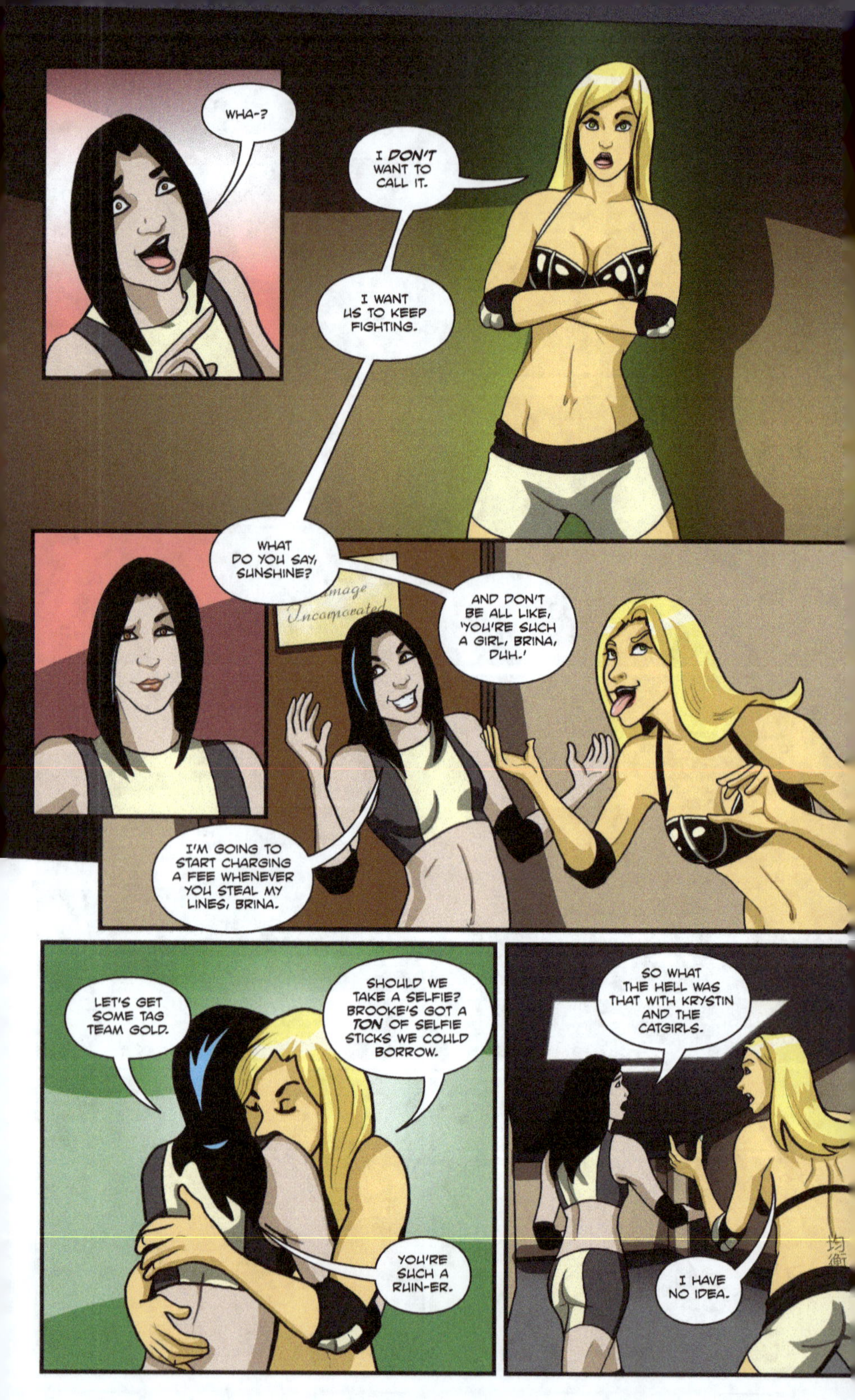

WHA-?
I DON'T WANT TO CALL IT.
I WANT US TO KEEP FIGHTING.
WHAT DO YOU SAY, SUNSHINE?
AND DON'T BE ALL LIKE, 'YOU'RE SUCH A GIRL, BRINA, DUH.'
I'M GOING TO START CHARGING A FEE WHENEVER YOU STEAL MY LINES, BRINA.
LET'S GET SOME TAG TEAM GOLD.
SHOULD WE TAKE A SELFIE? BROOKE'S GOT A TON OF SELFIE STICKS WE COULD BORROW.
YOU'RE SUCH A RUIN-ER.
SO WHAT THE HELL WAS THAT WITH KRYSTIN AND THE CATGIRLS.
I HAVE NO IDEA.

LATER THAT NIGHT.
EXCUSE ME, MA'AM? WE'RE ABOUT TO CLOSE UP.
OH SURE.
I JUST NEED TO PAY FOR THESE.
RETHiNKiNG NARCiSSiSM
How to Win Friends & Influence People
Aikido
HAVE A NICE NIGHT!
...
I'LL SEE WHAT I CAN DO.
End chapter 2

RIVAL ANGELS
CHAPTER 3
THE PRICE OF DREAMS

LADIES, IF YOU CAN PICK YOUR FIRST OPPONENT, WHO WOULD IT BE?
I'LL FIGHT ANYONE HERE. START THE TALLY.
I'D LIKE TO FIGHT SARA VALENTINE BECAUSE I THINK WE'D HAVE AN AWESOME MATCH.
WHOEVER GABRIELLE WANTS ME TO FIGHT. I TRUST THE MATCHMAKERS TO PUT ME IN A MATCH THAT THE FANS WILL LOVE.
DOESN'T MATTER. WHOEVER'S HOLDING MY BELT AT THE TIME.
RIVAL ANGELS UNCOVERED

WHAT? IF SOMEONE PUTS A MIC IN YOUR FACE AND ASKS WHO YOU WANT TO FIGHT, YOU ALWAYS SAY, "THE CHAMP." WHY ELSE ARE YOU HERE?
I WANT TO BE A CHAMPION, BUT I KNOW I NEED TO WORK MY WAY UP—
DAMN RIGHT.

YOU SPENT HOW LONG IN DEVELOPMENTAL? 3 MONTHS?
THAT'S IT?

DID YOU DO ANYTHING...UH, 'EXTRA' TO GET OUT EARLY?

LIKE WHAT?
RIVAL A UNCO

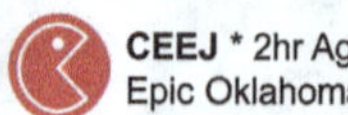 **CEEJ** * 2hr Ago   8: LIKE   REPLY
Epic Oklahoma Roll! #Can'tWinTheBigONe

 **Chavez Darwint** * 2hr Ago   10: LIKE   REPLY
Brenda had to resort to dectpion, confusion and trickery to squeak out the win.

 **CEEJ** * 1hr Ago   5: LIKE   REPLY
Brenda has nothing to prove to that blonde bimbo

 **Under Taker24*** 3hr Ago   0: LIKE   REPLY
Brenda will piece Sabina.

 **Evenflow** * 2hr Ago   5: LIKE   REPLY
Wow! Bitter much? Sabrina is the future.
Get outta the way, Dinosaur Brenda!"

 **Mr. Logic** * 2hr Ago   4: LIKE   REPLY
Anybody else think it's just a matter of time until Cote destroys the roster?

Under Taker24* 3hr Ago   1: LIKE   REPLY
Who?

IVORY TOWER * 3hr Ago   4: LIKE   REPLY
The Professor's lessons will be harsh and nobody will make the grade.

 **Kat's Tears** * 2hr Ago   3: LIKE   REPLY
Rua Ivory Tower'd her way into a #1 contender's match.
How many does that make now?

 **AC*** 3hr Ago   1: LIKE   REPLY
What a mark.

 **Kung Fu Naki** * 4hr Ago   4: LIKE   REPLY
Krystin needs to change her name to Judas!!!

 **Leo Tastic** * 4hr Ago   2: LIKE   REPLY
How can you judge her? You don't know the pressure she's under.

 **Kung Fu Naki** * 2hr Ago3: LIKE   REPLY
I know she's the definition of two-faced."

 **Wedgiesock** * 4hr Ago   9: LIKE   REPLY
The age of Aphrodite is just beginning! A belle is just a wannabe goddess!

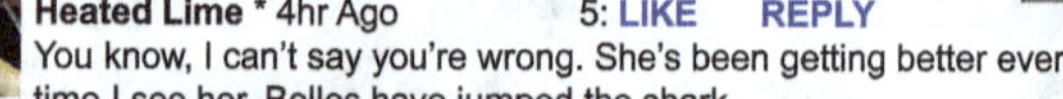

 **Heated Lime** * 4hr Ago   5: LIKE   REPLY
You know, I can't say you're wrong. She's been getting better every time I see her. Belles have jumped the shark.

Tricep Meat * 2hr Ago 3: LIKE   REPLY
Jumped the shark" has jumped the shark, but the Belles are definitely old news."

Season 3
Chapter 3

Art: Alan Evans
Story: Alan Evans and Justin Riley
Color Assists: Aaron Daly
Rival Angels created by Alan Evans
www.RivalAngels.com

MONDAY NIGHT.
WHERE DID NEVEAH GET HER EXTENSIONS? THE HORSE FACTORY? CLIP-IN OUTLET?
RIVAL ANGELS
BRAK!
SHE SHOULD'VE GONE TO 'HAIR GODDESS.' THAT'S RIGHT, THE 'DOUBLE D GODDESS' ALSO GOES TO 'HAIR GODDESS.' WHERE ELSE WOULD I GO?
AND AFTER THE SHOW TONIGHT, COME ON OUT TO 'TILTED SKIRT,' WHERE ME, SUN AND SABRINA WILL BE GETTING SOME BREW AND WINGS ON.
WE ARE-?
AGH!
KRAK!
SABRINA MIGHT NEED TO GO SEE DR. ISSAC OVER ON PROSPECT STREET-
WHY DON'T YOU COOL IT WITH THE RUNNING INFOMERCIALS?
WHY DON'T YOU TRY A BREATH MINT AND DEODORANT, POM POMS? THERE'S AN 'ULTA' DOWN THE BLOCK.
UL-?

-TA?
KRAK
WHACK!!!
UHNGH!
1...
2....
3
WHAT'S THAT ON YOUR FACE?
HEH.
ARE WE GOING FOR WINGS AFTER THIS?
WHAT IS WITH YOU AND FINGER FOOD?
I KNOW IT HURTS, YOU SIMPLE TWIT.
BACK OFF, D-LIST.

IT'S DOUBLE-D BUT I CAN UNDERSTAND YOUR FIXATION WITH THEM.
GREEN WITH ENVY.
LOOK, BRAIN DEAD, I'LL—
YOU'LL WHAT? I ALREADY KICKED YOUR ASS IN THE CENTER OF THE RING. MADE YOU TAP LIKE CHANNING TATUM.
THAT WAS A TAG MATCH. YOU WANT TO GIVE IT A GO, ONE-ON-ONE?
I'D BE HAPPY TO SCHOOL YOU...
LIKE THE ACADEMY OF HIGHER LEARNING-ROSEMONT/CHICAGO.
YOU GOT A LESSON COMING YOUR WAY NEXT WEEK.

GRAND OPENING
LET THE SAVINGS BEGIN!

THIS IS THE ONLY MONSTER THAT GETS NEAR MY PEARLY WHITES.

LEO!

WHY AM I DOING ALL OF THESE ENDORSEMENTS IN ONLY MY BIKINI?
WHAT? YOU HAVE A BEAUTIFUL BODY. EVEN THE ROCK HAD TO SHOW SKIN TO GET AHEAD.

YOU'RE PAYING YOUR DUES, KID.

IT SEEMS LIKE I'M ALWAYS PAYING MY DUES.

CHIN UP, KID.
I GOT A GIG FOR YOU HOSTING THE CHICAGO COLOR RUN.
THEY'RE BIG FANS OF YOU AND RIVAL ANGELS.

THAT'S GREAT!
WHAT'S A 'COLOR RUN?'

"IT'S THIS NON-COMPETITIVE 3 MILE RACE WHERE YOU GET DIFFERENT COLORED DUST DUMPED ON YA, AT DIFFERENT POINTS OF THE RACE."
"AFTERWARDS, EVERYONE GETS TOGETHER AND GETS MORE COLORED STUFF DUMPED ON 'EM."
THE HAPPIEST 5K ON THE PLANET!
START
THE COLOR RUN.

NON-COMPETITIVE? WHY IS IT EVEN A 'RACE' THEN?
F***IN' MILLENNIALS.

DO I GET TO WEAR CLOTHES?
WHATEVER YOU WANT, AS LONG AS IT'S WHITE.

I'LL HOST THE HELL OUT OF THIS. MAKE JON STEWART LOOK LIKE PARIS HILTON.

YOU SURE YOU GOT TIME FOR THIS, BROOKE-LYN? I SEE YOU GOT CHALLENGED BY THAT DROW CHEERLEADER GIRL.
PSSH. YEAH.

I GOT THIS.

MMA ACADEMY
KRYSTIN?

YEAH, I THOUGHT THAT WAS YOU.
WHAT BRINGS YOU TO AIKIDO TRAINING?
I HAVEN'T SEEN YOU SINCE THE FOOTBALL GAME.

EXPANDING MY HORIZONS, MERCY. IS THAT OKAY?
SORRY. THAT WAS BITCHY. I'VE BEEN TRYING TO BE LESS SO. OLD HABIT, Y'KNOW?

SURE.
HEARD ABOUT YOU AND TOPHER. SORRY.

IT'S FINE. LOOK, I'VE NO RIGHT TO ASK YOU BUT—
HE WON'T HEAR ABOUT IT FROM ME.

SO LONG AS YOU BUY THE FIRST ROUND AFTER CLASS.

UH... WELL...I HAVE TO...
YOU KNOW WHAT? OKAY.

MONDAY NIGHT.
YAAAAAYYY!!
BROOKE HAS BEEN IN CONTROL OF THE CHEERLEADER FOR A WHILE NOW.
RIVAL ANGELS

THUD!
SERISETTE WENT DOWN LIKE A SACK OF DOORKNOBS.
THIS IS UNCALLED FOR, JEFF.
IN THE ROPES! BREAK THE HOLD!
GOTTA DISAGREE WITH YOU ON THIS ONE. BECAUSE YOU'RE WRONG.
WHY? I'M SHOWING OFF HER GOOD SIDE.
BROOKE...!

YEAH, THAT'S NOT MY NAME.
SIGH. APHRODITE...!

SERISETTE IS IN A BAD WAY HERE.
SHE'S ABOUT TO BE THROWN FROM MOUNT OLYMPUS.

BAMM!
SERISETTE'S LOOKING LIKE LINDSAY LOHAN'S CAREER.

THAT'S AN ARROGANT PIN.
1....
2....
CONFIDENT, DAWN. CONFIDENT.

WHAT'S WITH THE SLOW COUNT, REF?
THAT'S NOT MY NAME.
IS YOUR NAME, 'JERK-FACE SLOW-COUNT?'

SHUT UP!
IT'S BREAK UP TIME.
SERISETTE IS TRYING TO FIGHT OFF APRHRODITE'S FINISHER!
THAT'S BLASPHEMY, DAWN!
SWISH!
WHAT A BEAUTIFUL HURRICANRA-NA!
FLIP!
THAT'S BLASPHEMY TOO!
SERISETTE'S GOT BOTH LEGS HOOKED!
THIS IS ALL BLASPHEMY!!
1
2

3
YAAAYY!!
NOW YOU REMEMBER HOW TO COUNT?
THAT WAS THE WRONG DIVINE INTERVENTION.
SHE DID IT! VICTORY FOR THE CHEERLEADER.
YES, BIG MOUTH, HA! IN YOUR FACE.
THIS IS THE WORST DAY EVAR.
I KICKED YOUR BIG ASS!
THAT'S RIGHT, EGOMANIAC.
I'M GOING TO BE DOING BIKINI COMMERCIALS FOREVER.
WHAT A GREAT WIN BY SERISETTE!
APHRODITE HAS COME A LONG WAY, BUT OBVIOUSLY SHE'S GOT SOME WORK TO DO.
TIME FOR A COMMERCIAL BREAK!
SHE TOOK A TOUGH LOSS BUT SHE'LL REFOCUS HER EFFORTS AND BE BACK BETTER THAN BEFORE.

WHACK!!!
WHACK!!!
WHACK!!!

WHACK!!!
SABRINA.

SABRINA.
WHACK!!!

WHACK!!!
SABRINA!

WHAT'S UP, ULTRAGIRL?
WHAT DID THAT BAG EVER DO TO YOU?
WHACK!!!

...

IT'S A STUPID WAY TO LOSE.
WHACK!!!

AND YET, THERE ARE DUMBER WAYS TO LOSE.
SAY, BEING TOO AMPED UP ABOUT LAST MATCH AND NOT FOCUSED ON TODAY'S MATCH.

IT WAS JUST SO HUMILIATING, TRAVIS. I WANTED TO WIN SO BADLY.

HEY, A WORLD CLASS CHAMPION CAUGHT YOU IN THE MIDDLE OF HIGH CHAOS.

GUESS WHAT?
I BET THAT NEVER HAPPENS TO YOU AGAIN. YOU'LL SEE IT COMING AND KNOW HOW TO BEAT IT.
THAT'S PROGRESS.

SOMETIMES, IT TAKES A LOSS TO REINFORCE THE IMPORTANCE OF TECHNICAL REFINEMENT...
AND LEARNING THE CORRECT WAY TO ESCAPE BAD POSITIONS AND AVOID THEM IN THE FIRST PLACE...
ESPECIALLY WHEN IT COMES TO CRAFTY VETERANS.

WOW.
I'M TOTALLY STEALING THAT.
FIST BUMP!

I'M JUST AS MUCH TO BLAME. I SHOULD'VE REMEMBERED THAT BRENDA WAS THE LEGAL ONE.
NO... SUNSHINE...

YOUR NEXT MATCH IS AGAINST THE TOWERS OF TERROR AND IF YOU'RE NOT READY, THEY'LL EAT YOU ALIVE.
LITERALLY, I THINK. LUNA'S A ZOMBIE AFTER ALL.
NAH, SHE'S JUST AN UNCOORDINATED MORON.

NO MORE 'OKLAHOMA ROLLS,' OR FEELING SORRY FOR YOURSELF.
IF YOU WIN THIS MATCH, YOU'LL GET A TITLE SHOT AGAINST BLACK AND BLUE AT THE PAY-PER-VIEW.
I'M NOT GOING TO LIE. THE PRESSURE IS ON. TITLE SHOTS ARE PRECIOUS.

IT'S TIME TO STEP IT UP.
NO BRENDA. NO CATGIRLS. TOWERS OF TERROR.
ARE YOU READY?

DOES A BEAR SHIT IN THE WOODS?
YEAH IT DOES!

THAT WAS RHETORICAL, BRINA.
I'M PREGNANT, NOT STUPID.
THANK YOU.
NIKKI MIGHT NOT HAVE KNOWN THAT.
I'M JUST TRYING TO HELP YOU OUT.

CHICAGO COLOR RUN.
THE COLOR RUN
SO, WE'LL NEED YOU THE START THE RACE AND AFTERWARDS, BRING EVERYONE IN FOR THE 'CLEANING STATION.'
START

I SEE YOU'RE DRESSED FOR RUNNING.
I CAN DO 3 MILES IN MY SLEEP.

THAT'S GREAT. REMEMBER IT'S JUST FOR FUN.
YEAH, NO PROBLEM.

IT'S JUST THAT YOUR CO-HOST SEEMS REALLY COMPETITIVE.
MY WHAT?

YOUR CO-HOST SERISETTE.
START
START

LIKE HELL SHE IS.
BEEP!

LEO! WHY THE HELL IS SERISETTE HERE?
OH YEAH, THAT. THE SPONSORS REALLY LIKED WHAT THEY SAW OF BOTH OF YOU IN YOUR MATCH.
THEY THINK YOU'LL BOTH MAKE GREAT HOSTS.

SCREW THAT. IT WASN'T A 'HOSTESS ON A POLE' MATCH.
I'M OUTTA HERE...!
NO, YOU'RE NOT!

I WORKED TOO HARD TO GET YOU THAT SPOT AND IT'S WAY TOO EARLY IN YOUR CAREER TO START WALKING OFF THE JOB.

IF YOU WANT TO GAIN TRACTION IN YOUR CAREER, THIS IS HOW IT'S DONE.
THIS SUCKS.
BROOKE, JUST BE HOW YOU ALWAYS ARE IN FRONT OF A CAMERA.

AND WHAT IS THAT SUPPOSED TO MEAN?
IT MEANS, YOU BE YOU.

OH, HEY BROOKE.
HEY, SERI.

I WAS JUST TELLING EVERYONE ABOUT HOW I SCHOOLED YOU IN OUR MATCH.
GREAT. IT'S GOOD YOU FINALLY HAVE SOMETHING WORTH SAYING.

I WAS ALSO TELLING EVERYONE THAT WE SHOULD MAKE THIS RACE INTERESTING.
ME VS YOU.

YOU'RE GOING TO RACE ME...WEARING THAT?
HOW HARD CAN IT BE? YOU'RE WEARING A PUSH-UP BRA WITH A SPORTS BRA.

SURE.

HEY EVERYONE, READY TO GET DIRTY?!
WOOOOOOOOO!
YEAH, WHO CAME TO SEE ME KICK HER—
BWONG!!
LET'S GO!
YAAAYY!!

Adjust!
Align!
Pull!
PAP!

HUH?
Double D Goddess

YOU'RE WELCOME.

FINISH
THANKS.

NOT USED TO RUNNING A MARATHON IN A BIKINI?
NO, IT'S IMPOSSIBLE.
CLEANING
NAH, YOU JUST NEED SOME PRACTICE.

WELL, YOU WIN. GOOD RACE.
WHERE YOU GOING?

WHAT?
WE STILL HAVE AN AFTER PARTY TO HOST THE HELL OUT OF!

CHICAGO!
WOOOOOOOOO!
WHO WANTS TO GET DIRTY WITH US!!
WOOOOOOOOO!

WELCOME BACK TO MONDAY NIGHT MELTDOWN!
IF YOU'RE JUST TUNING IN, WE'VE HAD SOME GREAT MATCHES SO FAR.
RIVAL ANGELS
MONDAY NIGHT MELTDOWN
CAMILLE COTE CONTINUES WRECKING EVERYONE THAT GETS IN HER WAY.
CAMILLE WAS TOO MUCH FOR MONICA RUMBLE TONIGHT WITH THAT REVERSE INVERTED FIGURE FOUR.
WE HAVE A NEW TELEVISION CHAMPION!
VICTORIA BUCKINGHAM WAS ABLE TO ROLL UP XTINA CARPENTER FOR THE WIN.
THAT TITLE IS HOTLY CONTESTED AND THIS MATCH WILL CONTEND FOR MATCH OF THE YEAR.
STILL TO COME, WE HAVE CALLISTA QUINN VS DYNA MO CHEN, VERONICA SILVER VS. DANIELLE PERFECTION...
DEF TECH VS RAMPAGE, A HUGE TAG TEAM MATCH IN ULTRADRAGON VS THE TOWERS OF TERROR...
BUT FIRST WE HAVE APHRODITE VS ANGEL SOPRANO COMING UP NEXT!
GODDESS VERSUS ANGEL!

LATER.
APH-RO-DI-TE!
POUND!
APH-RO-DI-TE!
POUND!
POUND!
APHRODITE WAS OFF TO A GREAT START UNTIL ANGEL SOPRANO GROUNDED HER.
ANGEL HAS BEEN SURGICAL IN HER ATTACK.
APH-RO-DI-TE!
THERE'S BEEN A LOT OF BAD BLOOD BETWEEN APHRODITE AND HELL'S BELLES SINCE THEY UNCEREMONIOUSLY KICKED HER OUT.
AFTER APHRODITE'S LOSS TO SERISETTE, SHE MIGHT NOT BE READY FOR SOMEONE THE CALIBER OF ANGEL.
YOU'RE DOING IT! GO! GO! GO!
APH-RO-DI-TE!
APH-RO-DI-TE!
OH, COME ON NOW! AMANDA WASN'T DOING ANYTHING.
WRONG! SHE WAS INSPIRING APHRODITE ON.
THAT'S NOT AGAINST THE RULES, JEFF!
SHUT IT, SWIPE LEFT.
...NO...
WHAM!!
IT LOOKS LIKE THE PAIN FROM THAT FIGURE FOUR LEGLOCK IS TOO MUCH. I THINK SHE'S OUT!
THUD!
1...
THEY ARE REALLY TAKING IT TO AMANDA OUTSIDE.
HER DIVINE INSPIRATION IS ALL USED UP.
2...

CHECK THAT, DAWN. APHRODITE AVOIDS THE 3-COUNT!
YAAAYY!!

IF SHE CAN REACH THE ROPES, IT'LL FORCE ANGEL TO BREAK THE HOLD!

IT'S KRYSTIN MOLINE!
POW!
YAAAYY!!
APH-RO-DI-TE!
APH-RO-DI-TE!
APH-RO-DI-TE!
WHAT IS DEF TECH THINKING?
SHE'S TRYING TO EVEN THE ODDS!

APH-RO-DI-TE!
APH-RO-DI-TE!
APHRODITE REACHES THE ROPE!
YAAAAAYYY!!
GRAB
KRYSTIN BIT OFF MORE THAN SHE COULD CHEW.

BREAK THE HOLD OR I'LL DISQUALIFY YOU!
1
2
3
4
POW!
APH-RO-DI-TE!
APH-RO-DI-TE!
HOW ARE WE SUPPOSED TO KEEP TRACK OF ALL OF THIS ACTION?

ULTRADRAGON IS HERE!
YAAAYY!!
THIS IS JUST CHAOS NOW, DAWN.
TRAIN-WRECK!
KRASH
KRYSTIN DROPS JEN AND KAT!
BAM!
BAMM!
UGH!
ANGEL'S LOOKING TO FINISH THE MATCH!
KILLSHOT TIME! IF SHE HITS THIS, IT'S OVER FOR APHRODITE.
BOOOOOO!
HEY, BITCHES!
TAKE A LOOK AT YOUR 'GODDESS' NOW.
BOOOOOO!

APHRODITE IS TRYING TO FIGHT OUT HER PREDICAMENT!
SHE'S WIGGLING!

SHE'S GOT ANGEL TRAPPED!
1....
2....
3

APHRODITE DID IT!
THAT MEANS THAT SHE ONLY NEEDS TO FACE KAT SMITH IF SHE WANTS TO RESOLVE HER WAR WITH HELL'S BELLES.
FINE
YAAAAAYYY!!

SUN?!
SUN, I'M SO—
YAAAYY!!
FIST BUMP!
DON'T MAKE IT A THING.

BE SURE TO CHECK US OUT AT THE RED CARPET PREMIERE OF GIRAFFEICANE!
US?
IT LOOKS LIKE THE UPSTARTS ARE BACK ON THE SAME PAGE.
AND IT'S ALL BECAUSE OF THE DOUBLE-D GODDESS, APHRODITE!

TIME FOR A COMMERCIAL BREAK, WE'LL BE RIGHT BACK!

EARLIER WE SAW PROFESSOR SHANNON McCOURT PUT HER #1 CONTENDER SPOT ON THE LINE WITH FORMER CHAMPION, BRENDA RUA.
UNDER PROTEST, I MIGHT ADD!

IT WAS A GREAT MATCH, AND THE PROFESSOR PUT IN A VALIANT EFFORT BUT IT WASN'T ENOUGH.
SLAM!

SHANNON SHOWED UNCHARACTERISTIC BAD SPORTSMANSHIP.
SHE LOST HER CHAMPIONSHIP OPPORTUNITY IN A MATCH SHE NEVER WANTED. HOW WOULD YOU FEEL?

IT WAS A GOOD THING THAT THE CATGIRLS WERE MONITORING THE ACTION.
BUNCH OF NO GOOD BUSYBODIES!

THE BIGGEST SURPRISE WAS SHANNON'S NEW ALLIES, SARA VALENTINE AND LORETTA DIAZ.
I'M NOT SURPRISED THAT SHANNON IS TOO HOTT!

BRENDA WILL BE CHALLENGING TO REGAIN HER TITLE NEXT WEEK AT THE INFERNAL CONFLICT PAY-PER-VIEW!
YVONNE HAS ALREADY DEFENDED HER TITLE FROM BRENDA, AND NEXT WEEK WILL BE NO DIFFERENT.
IT WILL BE A FANTASTIC MATCH!
COMING UP NEXT, KRYSTIN MOLINE VS. RAMPAGE!
KEEP CALM AND WRESTLE

KRYSTIN VS. RAMPAGE
DING DING

BLOCK
RAMPAGE IS WASTING NO TIME IN STARTING THIS MATCH.

MY SOURCES TELL ME THAT KRYSTIN HAS BEEN PUTTING IN EXTRA TRAINING. AIKIDO, I BELIEVE.
THUD!

IT LOOKS LIKE SHE'S PUTTING THAT TO GOOD USE.

SHE'S GOING FOR THAT HIP TOSS AGAIN.
DEF TECH!
DEF TECH!
DEF TECH!

STRUGGLE!
STRUGGLE!
KRYSTIN MIGHT BE GASSED FROM HELPING BROOKE EARLIER AGAINST HELL'S BELLES.
SEE? THIS IS WHY IT DOESN'T PAY TO HELP ANYONE.

YYYAAAGGHHHH!!!
1.....
2.....
KICKOUT
KRYSTIN'S GOT SOME LIFE LEFT. SHE'S GOING TO NEED IT.

THIS IS A NEW TWIST ON KRYSTIN'S USUAL TEXAS CLOVERLEAF.

THAT IS AN INNOVATIVE SUBMISSION HOLD.
TAP!!
TAP!!
TAP!!
YAAAYY!!

DEF TECH IS SHOWING RESPECT TO HER OPPONENT.
A WASTE OF TIME IF YOU ASK ME.

KRYSTIN LOOKS LIKE SHE'S BACK ON TRACK.
THAT'S WHAT WINNING WILL DO FOR YOU.
YAAAYY!!

COMING UP NEXT, WE HAVE OUR HUGE TAG TEAM CONTEST TO DETERMINE THE #1 CONTENDERS.
I'M EXCITED FOR THIS MATCH. IT'S BEEN A LONG TIME COMING.
ALREADY IN THE RING IS ULTRADGRAON.
THEY'RE FAST, FAST, FAST AND HAVE UNCANNY TEAMWORK.
ULTRA
TOWERS OF TERRO
AND ACCOMPANIED BY THEIR MANAGER, JOHANN...
ZOMBIE LUNA AND LOVER LOLA, THE TOWERS OF TERROR!
HOW WOULD YOU LIKE TO HEAR, MOM, MY DATE'S HERE,' AND YOU SEE THEM COMING UP THE WALK?
AT LEAST SHE ALREADY ATE.
YEAH, I GOT ANOTHER COLOR FOR HER FACE.
THE ENERGY COMING OFF OF THESE TWO TEAMS COULD POWER CHICAGO FOR A DECADE.
REFEREE NATHANIAL MILLER MIGHT WANT TO GET A TENNIS UMPIRE CHAIR TO REF THIS MATCH.
HE'S LIABLE TO LOSE A LIMB IF HE GETS TOO CLOSE!
DING DIN

DURING THE MATCH.
ZOMBIE LUNA IS SHOWING UNBELIEVABLE STRENGTH.
SHE'S STRONGER THAN TRAIN SMOKE.

BOOOOOO!
GLURG!
GET OUT OF THERE, JOHANN! HE'S NOT PART OF THE MATCH!
CHOKE!
HE'S LIKE THE SIXTH MAN IN A BASKETBALL GAME, DAWN. INVISIBLE, TO THE REF, BUT CAN MAKE ALL THE DIFFERENCE.

BRAK!
SUN IS DEMONSTRATING THAT NINJA LIKE AGILITY.
DAREDEVIL CALLS HER TO FILL IN WHEN HE NEEDS A VACATION.

ULTRADRAGON IS IN TROUBLE!
IT WAS JUST A MATTER OF TIME BEFORE STRENGTH BEAT SPEED.
IF YOU'RE PITTING FAST AGAINST STRONG, YOU'VE GOT TO BE NEAR-PERFECT.
BECAUSE FAILURE MEANS BEING CAUGHT AND STOPPED REAL SUDDENLY.
1
2....

KICKOUT!
SUN ONLY MANAGED TO PROLONG HER PUNISHMENT.
YAAAYY!!

YAAAYY!!
ULTRADRAGON IS BACK WITH THEIR TRADEMARK TEAMWORK.
THUD!

CHOKE!
CHOKE!
THE REF IS LOSING CONTROL OF THIS MATCH!
LET'S BE REAL. SHE NEVER HAD CONTROL AND KNEW IT.
I DON'T KNOW IF LUNA'S CHOKING THEM TO BREAK THE HOLD OR JUST BECAUSE SHE CAN'T HELP HERSELF!

GROAN!
SUPERPLEX!
THUMP!
LIKE A NAIL THAT'S JUST BEEN HAMMERED.

WITH SUN NEUTRALIZED, THEY'RE GOING TO FINISH SABRINA OFF.
BOOOOOO!
SA-BRI-NA
TWUNK

SA-BRI-NA
1....
2....

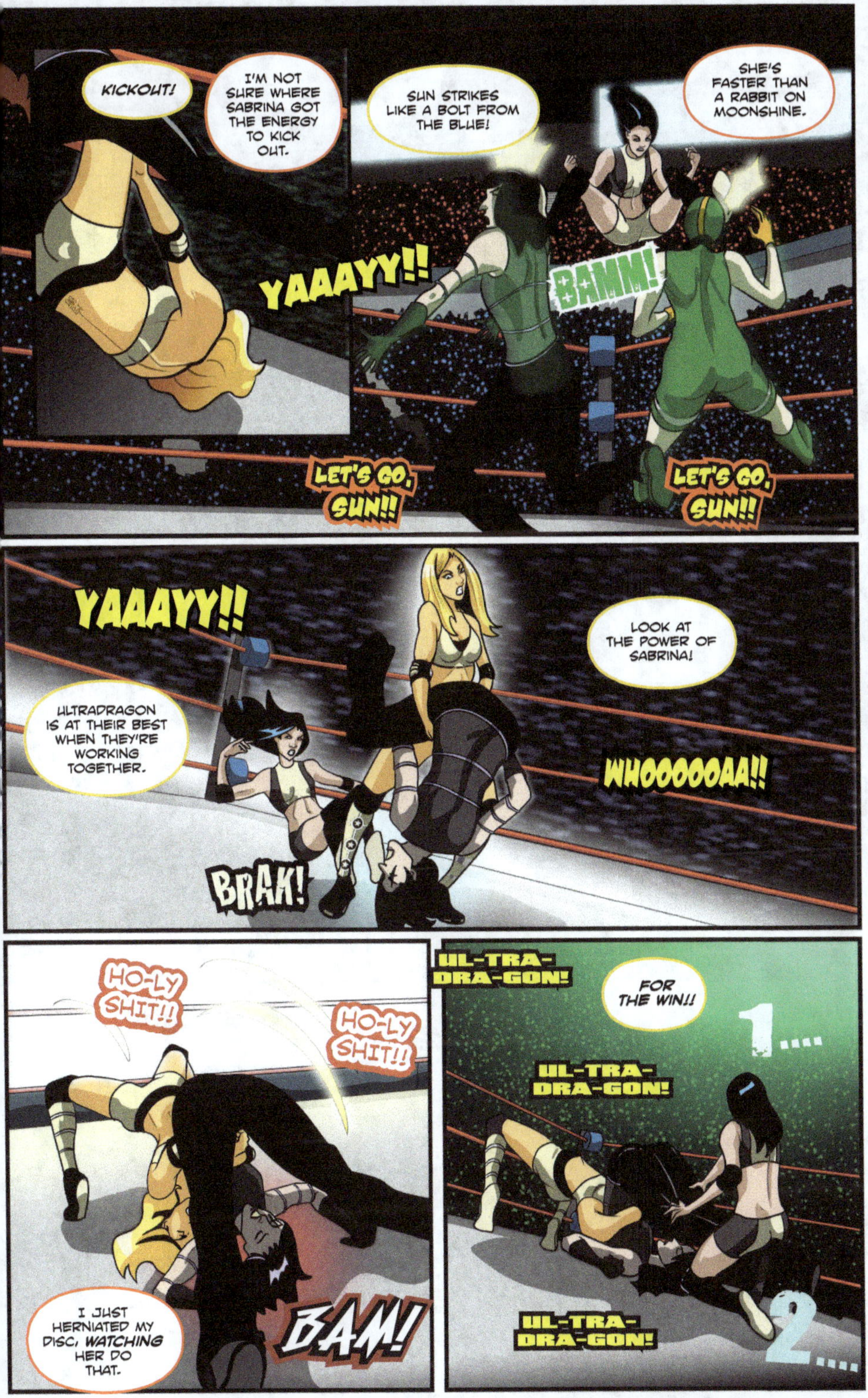

KICKOUT!
I'M NOT SURE WHERE SABRINA GOT THE ENERGY TO KICK OUT.
SUN STRIKES LIKE A BOLT FROM THE BLUE!
SHE'S FASTER THAN A RABBIT ON MOONSHINE.
YAAAYY!!
BAMM!
LET'S GO, SUN!!
LET'S GO, SUN!!

YAAAYY!!
ULTRADRAGON IS AT THEIR BEST WHEN THEY'RE WORKING TOGETHER.
LOOK AT THE POWER OF SABRINA!
WHOOOOOAA!!
BRAK!

HO-LY SHIT!!
HO-LY SHIT!!
I JUST HERNIATED MY DISC, WATCHING HER DO THAT.
BAM!

UL-TRA-DRA-GON!
FOR THE WIN!!
1.....
UL-TRA-DRA-GON!
UL-TRA-DRA-GON!
2.....

KICKOUT!
IT'S HARD TO KEEP A GOOD ZOMBIE DOWN.
GOOD? NO. ACCOMPLISHED, MAYBE.
SHOVE!
WHAT ARE THESE TWO PLAYING AT?
GREAT CATCH BY LOLA!
FLIP!
LUNA'S NOT A LAWN DART!
LOLA JUST TOMBSTONED HER OWN PARTNER!
KRAK!
KRAK!
THUD!
GROAN!
PPFFFFFITTTTTT!
KRAK!
THIS IS AWE-SOME!
THIS IS AWE-SOME!
THIS IS AWE-SOME!
ULTRAKICK!!
NINJA'D!!

POW!
KRASH
TSUNAMI!!!
1...
2....
3
YAAAAAYYY!!
UL-TRA-DRA-GON!
ULTRADRAGON DID IT! THEY'RE THE #1 CONTENDERS FOR THE TAG TEAM CHAMPIONSHIP.
UL-TRA-DRA-GON!
AMAZING MATCH.
GIMMIE A MIC!
UL-TRA-DRA-GON!

I DON'T KNOW ABOUT YOU BRINA, BUT I'M GASSED.
THAT MAY HAVE BEEN THE HARDEST MATCH WE'VE EVER WON.
BUT OUR HARDEST MATCH IS YET TO COME.
WE'VE SUFFERED SOME SETBACKS ALONG THE WAY, BUT WE'RE A BETTER TEAM FOR IT.
WOOOOOOOO!
WOOOOOOOO!
WOOOOOOOOO!
AND NEXT WEEK, WHEN WE FACE BLACK AND BLUE FOR THE TAG TEAM TITLES, THEIR TEAM NAME'S GONNA MEA-
WE WON'T HAVE TO WAIT UNTIL NEXT WEEK TO HEAR WHAT THE TAG CHAMPS HAVE TO SAY.
ULTRADRAGON HAD BETTER HOPE THAT THE CHAMPS ARE IN A GOOD MOOD!
THEY'RE NEVER IN A GOOD MOOD!
RIVAL ANGEL

NICE JOB GIRLS, BUT WE'RE NOT LETTING OUR BELTS GO FOR A GOOD LONG TIME.
BOOOOOOOOOO!!!!
WE CAN'T BE STOPPED. WE'VE BEATEN EVERY SINGLE TAG TEAM IN THIS DIVISION AT LEAST TWICE—
NOT US.
OOOOOOHHHHHHHH!
LOOK AT THE BIG BRAIN ON, BLONDE GIRL.
ITS ULTRA-GIRL. DON'T WORRY, YOU'LL GET IT.
YEAH, YOU GOT ONE LUCKY WIN, AND THEN WE KICKED YOUR ASSES THE NEXT.
NEXT WEEK, WE'LL DO IT AGAIN JUST TO CLEAR UP ANY MISCONCEPTIONS.
BUT, YOU TWO MAKE A GREAT TEAM. WE SHOULD KNOW.
WE'RE NOT TAKING YOU LIGHTLY.
SAVE IT. YOUR PRAISE MEANS NOTHING, BECAUSE YOU'RE SECOND-BEST.
THE ULTRADRAGON ERA STARTS NEXT WEEK.
YAAAAAYYY

IT'S BEEN A LONG WEEK. WHY ARE WE DOING THIS AGAIN?
IT'S GOOD FOR OUR 'BRAND,' SUN.
BROOKE, YOU'RE KIND OF BANGED UP. YOUR KNEE-
THIS IS OPENING UP DOORS.
CHICAGO
GIRAFFECANE
BROOKE, WHAT'S WITH THE SUNGLASSES?
FLASH!
FLASH!
FLASH!
FLASH!
FLASH!
THESE VERSACES WERE A GIFT FROM MY GOOD FRIEND DONATELLA.
FLASH!
FLASH!
FLASH!
GIRAFFEICANE. THIS IS GOING TO BE HORRIBLE.
I KNOW! IT'S GOING TO BE AWESOME.
I COULD USE A GOOD LAUGH THAT DOESN'T INVOLVE RUA'S FACE.
SWEET MERCY, MY FEET HURT.
MY EYES HURT FROM WATCHING THIS GARBAGE.
* SNORE *
MISS, YOUR PHONE...
END CHAPTER 3

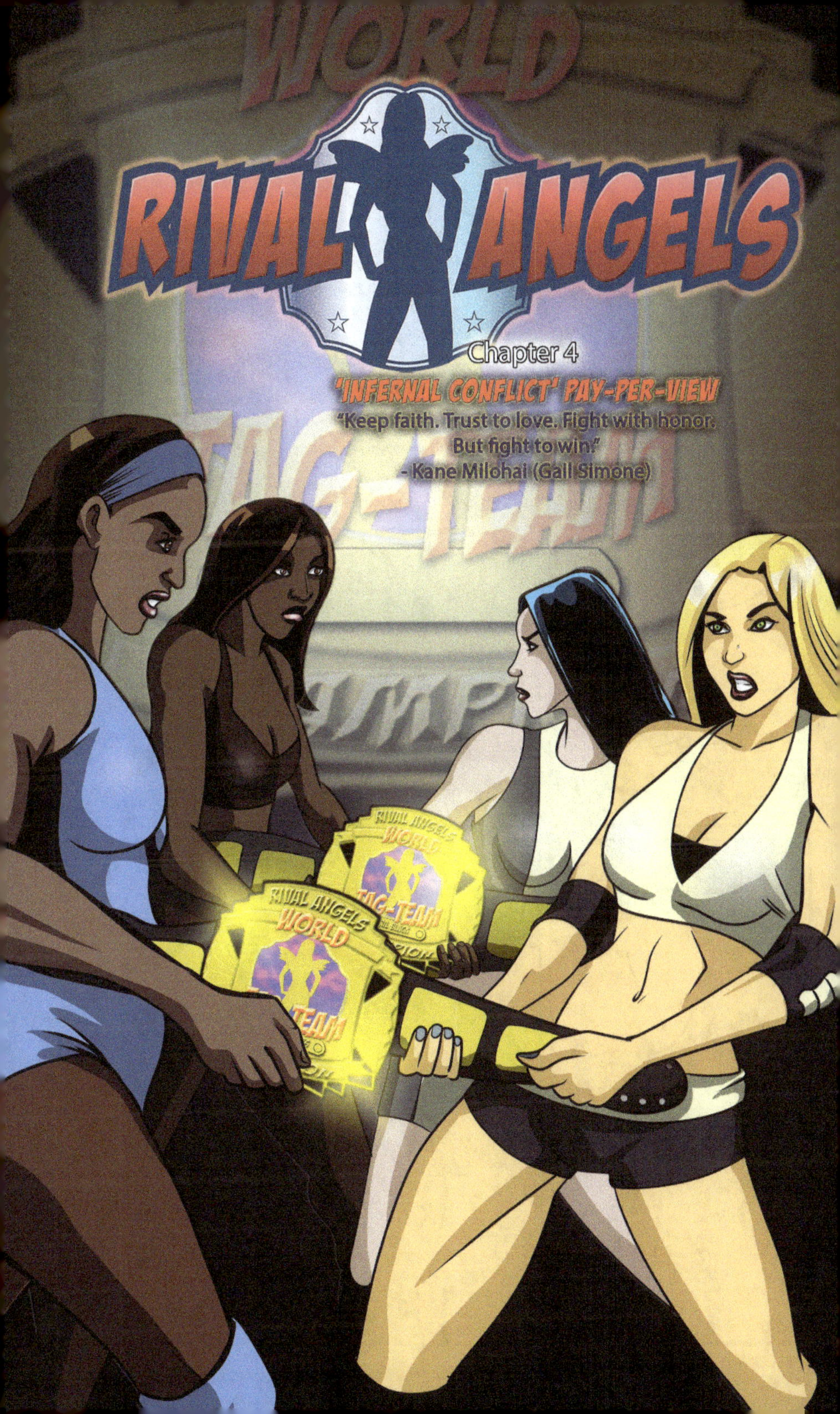

WORLD
RIVAL ANGELS
Chapter 4
'INFERNAL CONFLICT' PAY-PER-VIEW
"Keep faith. Trust to love. Fight with honor.
But fight to win."
- Kane Milohai (Gail Simone)
RIVAL ANGELS WORLD TAG-TEAM
RIVAL ANGELS WORLD TAG-TEAM

RIVAL ANGELS UNCOVERED
RIVAL A
LADIES, WE'VE CREATED AN ICE CREAM LINE TO GO ALONG WITH YOUR PERSONALITIES. HOW ABOUT IT? DO YOU THINK WE GOT IT RIGHT?
'ULTRAGIRL SALTY CARAMEL!' EVERYONE LOVES SALTY CARAMEL,
THEY CAN'T HELP IT.
ULTRAGIRL Y CARAM ICE CREAM
'DRAGON PISTACHIO AND HONEY.' YEP, YOU GOT ME IN A BOX. OR BUCKET. WHATEVER.
DRAGON ICE
'DEF TECH ROXBURY ROAD?' YEAH IT'S GOOD, BUT WHY ISN'T MY NAME BIGGER?
DEF TECH XBURY ROA ICE CREAM
WHAT THE HELL IS 'AUSSIE YLANG YLANG?' THAT'S BEATNIK TALK!
AUSSIE ANG YLA ICE CREAM
PUNT!
AGH!
IT'S LIKE A HUNK OF ICE!

**Heated Lime** * 1hr Ago   7: LIKE   REPLY
Aphrodite's been making the rounds with commercials, Color Run and Girafficane.

    Wedgiesock * 1hr Ago   11: LIKE   REPLY
    Beautiful. More Aphrodite is always good, or less if you know what I'm saying. #datdress

        Tricep Meat * 2hr Ago   3: LIKE   REPLY
        Serisette pinned Aphrodite. HAHA. #Jobber4liffe

Chavez Darwint * 2hr Ago   10: LIKE   REPLY
I heard the Upstarts have reunited.

Under Taker24 * 2hr Ago   1: LIKE   REPLY
I heard Ultradragon is going to break up. #CantWinTheBig1

    Melatonin * 2hr Ago   8: LIKE   REPLY
    Right, before their Tag Team Title match? GTFO Troll.

Chick Hera * 3hr Ago   4: LIKE   REPLY
Catgirls > Ultradragon #CantWinTheBig1

    Das * 3hr Ago   9: LIKE   REPLY
    Catgirls suck harder than Ultradragon. Agreed.

        OldWrestlingFan * 2hr Ago   7: LIKE   REPLY
        Ultradragon beat Towers of Terror. They comin' fo' dem beltz Black + Bleu.

Leo Tastic * 4hr Ago   7: LIKE   REPLY
Def Tech been leveling up. #Aikido

    AC * 3hr Ago   1: LIKE   REPLY
    Is that like Zika?

GEE MAN * 4hr Ago   5: LIKE   REPLY
Why is no one talking about Victoria's awesome TV Title win?

    CEEJ * 3hr Ago   5: LIKE   REPLY
    Because we want to see her fed to Camille.

        Zomaya * 3hr Ago   6: LIKE   REPLY
        Brenda would decimate Camille. Lmfao.

        Mr. Logic * 2hr Ago   4: LIKE   REPLY
        That's not how you use, '*decimate*.'

        Under Taker24 * 1hr Ago   5: LIKE   REPLY
        It's how you use your ma.

IVORY TOWER * 5hr Ago   0: LIKE   REPLY
Camille has had more matches this year than Brenda has the last two. One of those was because she HAD to squeeze Shannon out of her rightful spot.

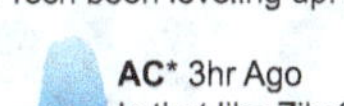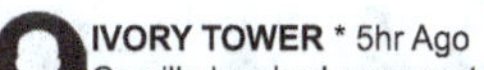

Season 3
Chapter 3

Art: Alan Evans
Story: Alan Evans and Justin Riley
Color Assists: Aaron Daly
Rival Angels created by Alan Evans
www.RivalAngels.com

INFERNAL CONFLICT PAY-PER-VIEW.
BLACK AND BLUE VS. ULTRADRAGON FOR THE WORLD TAG TEAM CHAMPIONSHIP.
JEFF, THE CHAMPS ARE GOING FOR THEIR FINISHER!
BLACK AND BLUE VS ULTRADRAGON
WORLD TAG TEAM CHAMPION
SUN'S ABOUT TO GET DECAPITATED!
THIS MATCH HAS HAD SO MANY TWISTS AND TURNS!
HOW DID WE END UP HERE, DAWN?

HOW WE GOT HERE.
SHE NEEDS TO TAG!
SABRINA'S BEEN IN THE RING FOR A LONG TIME.
IT'LL BE OKAY, SHE'S NOT EVEN FROM BOSTON!

THE TAG CHAMPS ARE WORKING LIKE A WELL-OILED MACHINE.
THEY'RE TAKING THEIR TIME IN BREAKING SABRINA DOWN.
AAAAGGHHH!

APRIL IS IN RESTRICTED AIRSPACE!
SHE'S LOOKING TO MAKE A MESS OF SABRINA'S FACE!
CRUSH!!
GROAN!
HEY, WONG!
THIS ONE'S FOR YOU, BITCH.
OOOOOOHHHHHHH!

AGH!
WHAT THE-?
KRAK!
TALK $H*T NOW.
YAAAYY!!

SABRINA, WITH THE QUICK THINKING COUNTER.
SHE MIGHT HAVE BOUGHT HERSELF SOME TIME TO RECOVER.
TWUNK
UHNG---!

LOOK! SABRINA'S ALMOST CLOSE ENOUGH TO MAKE THE TAG!
OUT, DANVERS!!
YOUR 5-COUNT WAS OVER HALF A MINUTE AGO!
THE REF IS TRYING TO REGAIN SOME CONTROL HERE.
SA-BRI-NA!
SA-BRI-NA!
SA-BRI-NA!

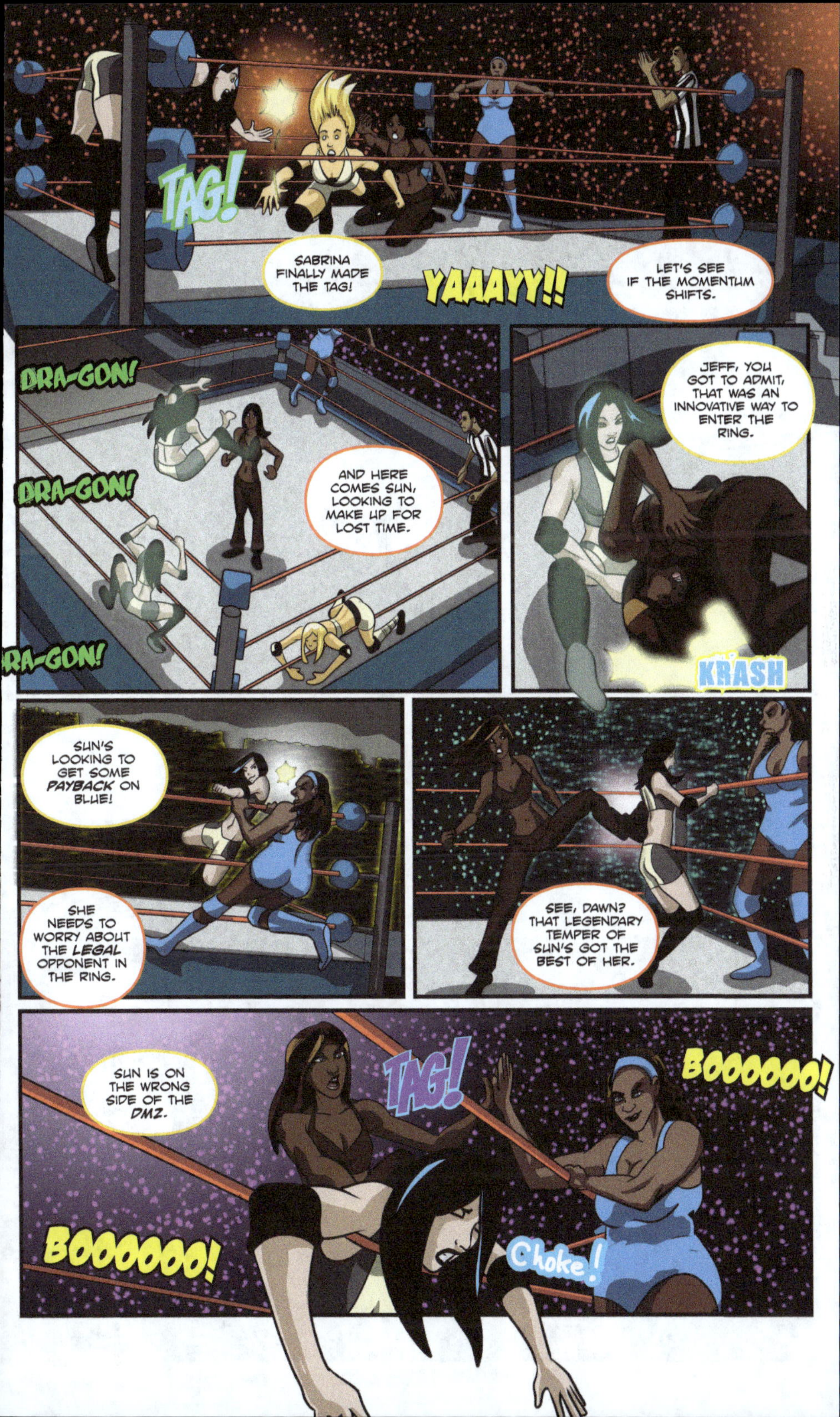

TAG!
SABRINA FINALLY MADE THE TAG!
YAAAYY!!
LET'S SEE IF THE MOMENTUM SHIFTS.
DRA-GON!
DRA-GON!
RA-GON!
AND HERE COMES SUN, LOOKING TO MAKE UP FOR LOST TIME.
JEFF, YOU GOT TO ADMIT, THAT WAS AN INNOVATIVE WAY TO ENTER THE RING.
KRASH
SUN'S LOOKING TO GET SOME PAYBACK ON BLUE!
SHE NEEDS TO WORRY ABOUT THE LEGAL OPPONENT IN THE RING.
SEE, DAWN? THAT LEGENDARY TEMPER OF SUN'S GOT THE BEST OF HER.
SUN IS ON THE WRONG SIDE OF THE DMZ.
TAG!
BOOOOOO!
BOOOOOO!
Choke!

IT LOOKS LIKE BLACK AND BLUE ARE LOOKING FOR A SUN SET.

NOW.

IT'S ALL OVER FOR ULTRADRAGON-!

SUN'S ABOUT TO GET DECAPITATED!

UHNF!

THUMP

WHERE DID SABRINA COME FROM?

IS SHE MENTAL? SHE COULD'VE CRIPPLED THE BOTH OF THEM!

HO-LY SHIT!!

KRASH

IT...WAS... WORTH IT.

HO-LY SHIT!!

HO-LY SHIT!!

THIS IS AWE-SOME!

I HAVE SEEN SOME RIDICULOUSNESS IN MY TIME...

SO YOU OWN A MIRROR?

WHA-?

THIS IS AWE-SOME!

THIS IS AWE-SOME!

KICK!
SUN COMES TO LIFE!
THAT SNEAKY NINJA NEEDS TO GET OFF THE CHOPPING BLOCK!
HEY!

I HATE YOUR...
KNOBBY KNEES!
BAMM!
YOUR STUPID FACE!
AND YOUR TREE TRUNK LEGS!
KICK!
YANK!
TRYING TO KEEP UP WITH HER IS LIKE TRYING TO KEEP UP WITH USAIN BOLT, IF HE TALKED THAT MUCH SMACK, THAT IS.
JEFF, SHE'S A BLUR IN THERE!

APRIL LOOKS LIKE SHE'S RECOVERED FROM THE CRASH LANDING.
AND LOOKING TO DELIVER THE KILLING BLOW.
SUN'S LOOKING TO PUT THE BIG GAL TO SLEEP.
SABRINA TURNED IT AROUND!
THUD!
SQUEEZE
YAAAYY!!
YEAH, BUT DOES SHE HAVE ANYTHING LEFT TO TRY AND HELP HER PARTNER?

BLURGH.
THEY'RE GOING TO NEED A SOLUTION TO PEEL SUN OUTTA THERE.
CRUSH!!

UL-TRA-DRA-GON!
APRIL!
UL-TRA-DRA-GON!
UL-TRA-DRA-GON!

KRAK!
ULTRAKICK!
YAAAYY!!

LUNGBLOWER!
KRICK!
YAAAYY!!

BRINA?
...WHAT ARE YOU...?
BLUE IS STILL ON HER FEET!
GIVE 'EM, HELL.
WHAT IS SABRINA THINKING, DAWN?

....RRRRGGHHH....
SHE CAN'T DO IT...

WHOOOOOAA!!

MICHINOKU DRIVER!
BOOOM

1....
2....
3

PAAARTY!!
NEW CHAMPS!
HOW DID YOU DO THAT?!
NEW CHAMPS!
ULTRADRAGON ARE THE NEW TAG TEAM CHAMPIONS!
I DON'T KNOW.
THOSE STUPID DEADLIFTS THAT NIKKI MAKES US DO?
YOU DESERVE IT
YOU DESERVE IT
YOU DESERVE IT
YOU DESERVE IT
YOU DESERVE IT

CONGRATULATIONS.
THANK YOU.
MINE!!!
SNATCH!
YAAAY!!
YOU DESERVE IT
YOU DESERVE IT
YOU DESERVE IT
YOU DESERVE IT
YOU DESERVE IT
YEP.
YOU DESERVE IT
YOU DESERVE IT

LATER.
THIS MATCH HAS BEEN SURPRISINGLY EVEN THUS FAR.
DON'T TAKE APHRODITE FOR GRANTED. SHE'S GOT SKILLS THAT MATCH HER EXTREME HOTNESS.
YOUR ELOQUENCE KNOWS NO BOUNDS.
Kat Smith vs. Aphrodite

KAT IS STRETCHING APHRODITE LIKE A PELT.
YANK!
APH-RO-DI-TE!
SHE'S GOING TO RIP APHRODITE'S HEAD OFF!
STRETCH
AAAAAAAGH!
SCREAM FOR ME!
NO! THAT'S ONE OF MY FAVORITE PARTS!
APH-RO-DI-TE!
THUD!
KAT'S FACE LOST THE BATTLE WITH APHRODITE'S SIZE 13.
YAAAYY!!

CRUSH!!
AVALANCHE!
A HEAVENLY COLLISION!
WILL YOU STOP?
WOOOOOOOO!

THUMP!
KAT JUST LEVELED APHRODITE WITH THAT CLOTHESLINE!
YOU CAN NEVER COUNT KAT OUT.
THIS IS THE WRONG PART OF TOWN FOR APHRODITE.
FLIP!
APH-RO-DI-TE!
APH-RO-DI-TE
APHRODITE IS TAKING IN SOME RARIFIED AIR.
APH-RO-DI-TE
KATASTROPHE!
GROAN!
BOOOM
HEAVEN FALLS!
1....
KAT'S GOT THIS.
BOOOOOO!
APHRODITE WAS ALMOST ABLE TO RUN THE TABLES ON HELL'S BELLES.
2....

1....
2....
3
WHAT IS THIS?
HOLY CRAP, HOW DID SHE DO IT?
DIVINE INSPIRATION, DAWN! IT'S THE ONLY THING THAT MAKES SENSE!

YAAAAAYYY!!
NO NO NO NO NO...
OW OW OW OW
APH-RO-DI-TE!
APH-RO-DI-TE!
APH-RO-DI-TE!

NO!
THIS IS ALL WRONG!
YOU'RE DEAD, LENNOX! NEXT TIME, IT'LL GO HOW IT SHOULD!

IS THAT REALLY WHAT YOU WANT?

WHAT?
DON'T YOU HAVE ANYTHING BETTER TO DO? GO GET A BELT OR SOMETHING.
I'VE GOT PLANS OTHER THAN FIGHTING HELL'S BELLES. I'M SO OVER YOU BEATNIKS.
MY STAR POWER IS GREATER THAN ALL OF YOURS PUT TOGETHER.
I'M GOING TO BE A BIG STAR IN RIVAL ANGELS. I'M GOING TO BE A BIG THING IN THIS WORLD.
SHE'S NUTS.
LET'S GO, BOSS.
.........UGH.
I AM THE HOT CHOCOLATE SOUFFLE OF PROFESSIONAL WRESTLING!
ER: APHRODITE
APH-RO-DI-TE!
APH-RO-DI-TE
APH-RO-DI-TE!

3-WAY DANCE

CAMILLE COTE
VS AMANDA BREAKER
VS RAMPAGE

THIS IS NOT GOOD.

OOOOOOHHHHHHH!

AND JUST LIKE THAT, CAMILLE COTE MAKES SHORT WORK OF HER COMPETITORS.

TAP!! TAP!!

APPLAUSE

HOLD ON.

IT'S NOT OVER, DAWN.

I'M NOT LETTING GO UNTIL YOU TAP!

NOW I'M VICTORIOUS.

VICIOUS!

AND AMAZING!

FINE, FINE, FINE! IT HURTS!

TAP!! TAP!! TAP!!

KRYSTIN MOLINE VS DANIELLE PERFECTION
DANIELLE HAS HELD KRYSTIN UP THERE A LONG TIME.
KRAK!
AGREED.
OUCH!
THE VIEW ISN'T WORTH THE CRASH.
THE DEFINITION OF TECHNICIAN GUTTED IT OUT AND GOT THE WIN!
TAP!!
TAP!!
TAP!!
AMAZING RECOVERY BY DEF TECH.
YES.
SHE MUST BE HURTING IF SHE NEEDS HELP GETTING INTO THE BACK.
SHE GOT BACK FROM AN INJURED HAND NOT TOO LONG AGO.
HERE'S HOPING SHE AVOIDS IT ALTOGETHER THIS TIME.

BRENDA RUA VS YVONNE CARMICHAEL FOR THE WORLD CHAMPIONSHIP.
YAAAAAYYY!!
THIS SHOULD BE A BATTLE FOR THE AGES!
BRENDA IS SINGLE-MINDED IN TRYING TO GET HER BELT BACK. A SHAME THE CHALLENGER WILL COME UP SHORT AGAIN.
LASER FOCUSED. UNBEATABLE.
MY NAME IS GOLD, MY OUTFIT IS GOLD AND MY HAIR IS GOLD.
IT'S A STABLE OF GOLD!
YAAAYY!!
LATER.
GOLDNIGHT PEDIGREE!
LATER.
CELTIC HAMMER!
IS THIS THE END?!
IT SHOULD BE. SHE JUST NEEDS TO MAKE THE...
COVER! BRENDA NEEDS TO END THIS NOW!
IT CAN'T BE OVER! IT CAN'T!
LATER.
DING DING
WHAT NOW?! DON'T TELL ME WE'RE OUT OF TIME!
WELP, LOOKS LIKE YVONNE CARMICHAEL IS STILL YOUR CHAMPION OF THE WORLD.

RIVAL ANGELS
PRESS CONFERENCE
I DESERVE A REMATCH!
YVONNE'S NEXT WORLD TITLE DEFENSE WILL BE AGAINST CAMILLE COTE.
I DIDN'T LOSE THAT MATCH!
YOU DIDN'T WIN EITHER, HONEY.
HOW MANY CHANCES DO YOU NEED? LET SOMEONE ELSE HAVE A GO.
WHY DO YOU GET THE NEXT TITLE SHOT? WHAT HAVE YOU DONE?
THIS.
IT SAYS ONLY ONE OTHER PERSON IN THE WORLD BEAT ME, AND IT WASN'T YOU.
YOUR TIME IS OVER.
I LOVE ALL OF THIS ATTENTION FROM THE CHALLENGERS BUT YVONNE CARMICHAEL, THE GOLD STANDARD, WILL BE HANGING ON TO THIS BELT FOR A LONG TIME.
JUST LIKE ULTRADRAGON, THE NEW TAG TEAM CHAMPIONS ARE GOING TO REIGN FOR A LONG TIME.
BRONZE THE GOLD, CUZ THE NAMES ON THE PLATES AREN'T GONNA CHANGE.

LET'S TAKE SOME QUESTIONS.
KRYSTIN, DID YOU SUFFER AN INJURY IN YOUR MATCH WITH DANIELLE PERFECTION?

IT DOESN'T LOOK LIKE ANYTHING SERIOUS. NOTHING A FEW WEEKS OF REST WON'T FIX.
I'LL PROBABLY DO SOME REHAB AT THE MMA ACADEMY.

NEXT QUESTION.
ULTRADRAGON, HOW DOES IT FEEL TO BE THE BEST TEAM IN PRO WRESTLING?

WHAT DO YOU THINK?
OMG, I'VE...WE'VE BEEN WAITING FOR THIS OUR ENTIRE CAREERS-
RIVAL ANGELS WORLD TAG-TEAM CHAMPION

THEY'RE NOT THE BEST TEAM IN PRO WRESTLING.
RIVAL ANGELS WORLD TAG-TEAM CHAMPION

THEN WHY DON'T THEY HAVE THE BELTS?

BECAUSE THEY FIGHT THE BEST TEAMS. YOU FIGHT THE RIGHT MATCHUP.
BEING POPULAR DOESN'T MAKE YOU THE BEST.

THEY MAY HAVE THE BELTS BUT THEY'RE NOT THE BEST TEAM. THAT'S THE CATGIRLS, AND THOSE UPSTARTS HAVE NEVER BEATEN THEM.

THIS MAKES US THE BEST! GOLD, BITCH, SOMETHING YOU DON'T HAVE.
HART, MICHAELS, AUSTIN. ALL TAG CHAMPS BEFORE THEY WON WORLD TITLES!
YOU WANT TO TALK MATCHUPS? HOW ABOUT MY FOOT WITH YOUR FRONT TEETH? ULTRAKICK PARTY, AND YOU'RE INVITED.

FINE WITH ME. I'D TAKE THE BOTH OF YOUR BELTS IN A TWO-ON-ONE MATCH.
OOOOOOHHHHHHH!

DO YOU WANT A SHOVEL, RUA?
YOU JUST BURIED THE ENTIRE TAG TEAM DIVISION.
BRENDA WILL NOT BE CHALLENGING THE TAG TEAM CHAMPIONS.

CAUSE YOU KNOW I'D WIN.
SHE KNOWS YOU'D GET TORN APART. THEY'RE THE TAG CHAMPS.
SHE'S PROTECTING YOU. AGAIN. LOTS OF T-SHIRTS TO MOVE BEFORE THE WORLD REALIZES YOU'RE DONE.

YOU MIGHT THINK YOU'RE LIVING IN THEIR HEAD RENT-FREE, RUA...
BUT THE WINDS ARE GOING TO CHANGE ONE DAY, AND THEY'RE GOING TO REMEMBER HOW YOU TREATED THEM.

SCREW THAT, 'ONE DAY' NONSENSE. LET'S GO.

ULTRADRAGON'S FIRST TAG TEAM TITLE DEFENSE WILL BE HELD IN THE RING.
NEXT QUESTION?

WHAT'S NEXT FOR THE HOT CHOCOLATE SOUFFLE' OF WRESTLING?
THAT'S ME!

SOUNDS LIKE BOOBZILLA THINKS SHE'S TOO HOT.
ALLOW US TO DISABUSE YOU OF THAT THINKING.

ANY OF YOU SCRUBBERS WANT TO GIVE IT A SHOT, I'LL SHOW YOU WHY YOU NEED TO STEP UP OR STEP ASIDE! YOU CAN'T STOP MY GO.

THAT'S A MATCH WE'LL HAVE TO LOOK AT PUTTING TOGETHER.
NEXT QUESTION?
IS THERE ANY TRUTH TO THE RUMOR THAT-?
THERE'S NO TRUTH TO ANY RUMORS.
NEXT QUESTION.

AFTER THE VICTORY PARTY.
END CHAPTER 4

RIVAL ANGELS
Christmas Angels
Alan Evans
Dave Reynolds
Story
Art and Letters

Bankers Life Fieldhouse Arena
Indianapolis, IN
HOME COURT
THE REFEREE HAS LOST CONTROL OF THIS MATCH!
DAWN, THE REFEREE ONLY EVER HAD THE ILLUSION OF CONTROL.
IT WOULD BE HARD TO CONTROL ANY 2 OF THESE WOMEN IN THE BEST OF TIMES, AND THIS 8-WOMAN TAG IS NOT THE BEST OF TIMES, JUDGING BY THE PANICKED LOOK ON THE REF'S FACE!
IT'S A PIER 6 BRAWL OUTSIDE THE RING!
CANADIAN DESTROYER!
THAT'S GOTTA BE IT, JEFF!
KAT'S HEAD CRACKED LIKE AN EGG WITH A SIDE OF HAM THEY CALL BACON!
1...
2...
3!
YAAAAAAAAY

WHAT AN AMAZING MAIN EVENT, DAWN.
A GREAT CHRISTMAS VICTORY FOR THE UPSTARTS.
'The Lil Dragon,' Sun Wong
Sabrina 'Ultragirl' Mancini
'Aphrodite' Brooke Lennox
'The Definition of Technician' Krystin Moline
YAAAAAAAAAY
NICE JOB, SABRINA!
YEAH, YOU BROKE THE HOMETOWN CURSE.
I COULDN'T HAVE DONE IT WITHOUT YOU.
YOU'RE WELCOME.
THE WHAT NOW?
PICKING UP THE WIN IN YOUR HOMETOWN.
IT'S AS RARE AS A UNICORN OR SINGLE GUY NOT LIVING WITH HIS PARENTS.
LET'S NOT PUSH IT THEN. LET'S JUST LEAVE NOW!
WHAT'S THE RUSH, ULTRAGIRL?
IT'S CHRISTMAS! DON'T YOU WANT TO SPEND A LITTLE TIME WITH YOUR FAMILY?
TOTALLY, BUT I DON'T WANT TO BE LATE FOR THE NEXT SHOW. MOMENTUM AND ALL THAT.
THAT'S NOT UNTIL NEXT WEEK!
OH, SO CLOSE. SO DAMN CLOSE.
?

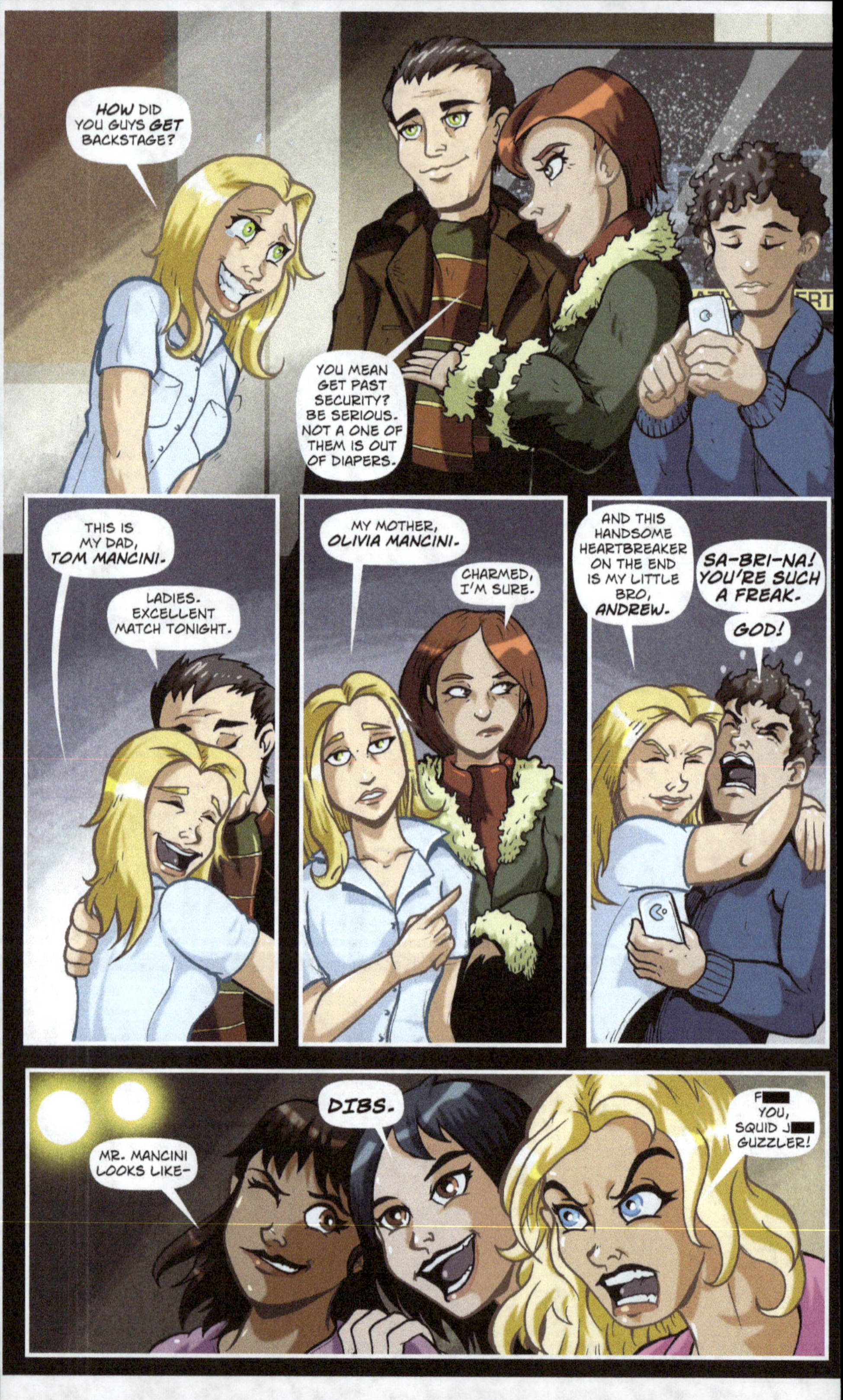

HOW DID YOU GUYS GET BACKSTAGE?
YOU MEAN GET PAST SECURITY? BE SERIOUS. NOT A ONE OF THEM IS OUT OF DIAPERS.
THIS IS MY DAD, TOM MANCINI.
LADIES. EXCELLENT MATCH TONIGHT.

MY MOTHER, OLIVIA MANCINI.
CHARMED, I'M SURE.

AND THIS HANDSOME HEARTBREAKER ON THE END IS MY LITTLE BRO, ANDREW.
SA-BRI-NA! YOU'RE SUCH A FREAK.
GOD!

MR. MANCINI LOOKS LIKE—
DIBS.
F▮ YOU, SQUID J▮ GUZZLER!

WELP! THANKS FOR COMING OUT, BUT IT'S TIME FOR US TO GET GOING.

GOTTA MAKE THAT RED EYE TO MINNESOTA, DONTCHA KNOW.
EVERE WEATHER A
YOU'RE NOT GOING ANYWHERE.

WHA- WHAT?
ALL FLIGHTS ARE CANCELED AND THE GOVERNOR HAS DECLARED A STATE OF EMERGENCY.
ALL ROADS ARE CLOSED AS OF 11PM.
LOOK, I'LL JUST GET A HOTEL ROOM WITH MY FRIENDS.
SABRINA... NO ROADS, NO UBER, NO STORES OPEN, NO HOTEL ROOMS.
STOP BEING RIDICULOUS.

YOU'LL COME HOME TONIGHT, SO LET'S GET GOING.

YES, YES, YOUR GIRLFRIENDS CAN STAY TOO.

EXIT
ER.
???
≈
YES, MOM.

Mancini Household
Still in Indianapolis
YOU LADIES CAN TAKE ANDREW'S ROOM.
ANDREW WILL BE SLEEPING ON THE COUCH.
≶MUMBLE≷ YOU'RE WELCOME ≶MUMBLE≷
IT'S REALLY VERY GENEROUS OF YOU ALL, MRS. MANCINI.
CALL ME, "OLIVIA," GIRLS.
YEAH, OLIVIA, THANK YOU...
...VERY ...MUCH.
SLEEP TIGHT, GIRLS.
SQUILSH SQUILSH
IS THAT A SOCK ON THE FLOOR?
EEEEWWW.
THIS IS NOT A WIN.

My Little Pony
Sabrina's Room
STAY AWAY!
I MEAN IT!
KNOCK KNOCK
CAN I COME IN?
IT'S OPEN.
WE'RE JUST GETTING READY FOR BED.
Beauty and the Beast
SO... ARE YOU TWO...
YES, WE'RE PARTNERS.
WE'RE WRESTLING TAG TEAM PARTNERS.
IT'S WHY I ALWAYS SLEEP IN THE NUDE. TAKE THAT, INDIANA!

...
WHAT DOES THAT EVEN MEAN?

OKAY LADIES, UM, HAVE A GOOD NIGHT.
I GUESS IT MAKES SENSE.

DUMMY.
BUMP
≶SNIRK≶

The next morning
HOW LONG HAS SHE BEEN OUT THERE?

AN HOUR AND COUNTING.
WHY IS SABRINA BEING A HEAD-CASE? HER MOM SEEMS NICE.

YOU REMIND ME OF MYSELF WHEN I WAS YOUNGER.
I GET THAT A LOT.

I DON'T KNOW. I GUESS THEY GOT A LOT OF HEAT FROM WHEN SHE WAS A KID.
HADOKEN!!

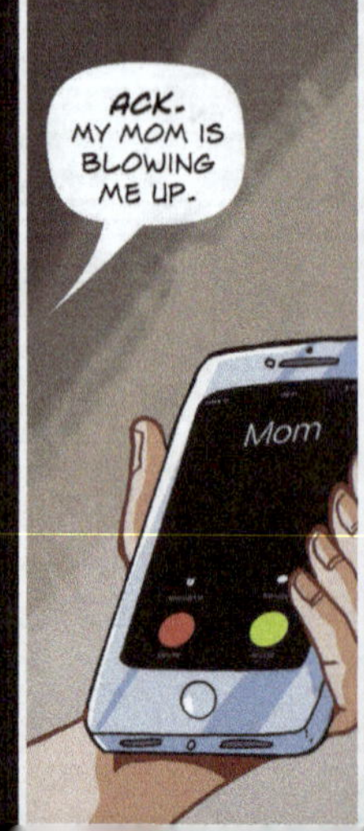

ACK. MY MOM IS BLOWING ME UP.
Mom

YOU'RE NOT GOING TO ANSWER HER?
WHO?
YOUR MOM!
WHY?

BECAUSE IT'S CHRISTMAS!
I'LL TEXT HER IN A LITTLE WHILE.
WHAT? YOU DON'T LIKE YOUR MOM EITHER?
HEY! I LIKE HER FINE.
I CALL HER MONTHLY.
UGH.
AND ME AND SABRINA AREN'T THE ONLY ONES.
BROOKE HASN'T SEEN HER MOM IN YEARS.
YEAH, BUT SHE'S IN AUSTRALIA.
SHE COULD STILL SKYPE OR SOMETHING, BUT SHE DOESN'T.
PROBABLY DOESN'T LIKE THE LIGHTING.
YOU BITCHES ARE ALL CRAZY.
WE'RE NOT CRAZY JUST BECAUSE WE AREN'T ALL 'GILMORE GIRLS.'
FWOOMPH

ELSA DONE HAULED OFF AND WHOOPED YOUR ASS?
COFFEE.
COFFEE FOR YOUR CHAMPION...
...OF SNOW SHOVELING.

STOP LOOKING AT THOSE. I NEVER AUTHORIZED THEM.

SINCE YOU'RE HERE, SABRINA, I'D LIKE TO TAKE SOME HOLIDAY FAMILY PICTURES.
??

...OH-KAY.
GREAT! I HAVE A DRESS YOU CAN WEAR.
ζSIGHξ
WHY DO I HAVE TO WEAR A DRESS YOU PICKED OUT?

BECAUSE OTHERWISE YOU'LL LOOK LIKE A WOMEN'S STUDIES MAJOR.
HEE HEE HEE
FINE. YOU NAG WORSE THAN THE COPS.

YOU DIDN'T GET ANY MORE TATTOOS DID YOU?
STILL WORKING ON THE SAMOAN TRIBAL TATTOO.
A GIANT ANIMATED MINI-SABRINA ETCHED ALL OVER MY BACK!
SHARK HEAD!!

YOU'RE KIDDING.
SOMEONE TELL ME SHE'S KIDDING!
SHE'S KIDDING, MRS. MANCINI.
THANK GOD, FOR SMALL MIRACLES.

SHARK HEAD?
IT'S A DISNEY THING.
OF COURSE IT IS.

YOU LOOK PRETTY!
I HAVE SOME EARRINGS THAT WOULD GO GREAT WITH THAT.
DON'T BOTHER.
OH, IT'S NO BOTHER.
SABRINA, HAVE YOU BEEN IN PRISON THAT I HAVEN'T BEEN AWARE OF?
MOM, WHAT? I'M WEARING THE STUPID DRESS!
I FORGOT YOU HAD MAN-SHOULDERS!
THEY'RE BIGGER THAN ANDREW'S!
NICE, MOM!
ANDREW DOES HAVE SMALL SHOULDERS, BUT THAT WAS AN NWA JIM CORNETTE FLASH PAPER BURN.
GUYS, LOOK AT THIS!
EEEEK!!
NO... IT CAN'T BE TRUE...
I HAVE TO ADMIT, I'M KIND OF DISAPPOINTED.
⋛SIGH⋚ MY HAPPIEST AND SADDEST MEMORY.

SABRINA, THIS IS SO AWESOME!
WHY DIDN'T YOU EVER TELL US?

SNATCH

I THREW THIS AWAY.
AND I HAD ANOTHER MADE. YOU FORGOT I HAD THE NEGATIVES.
THE WHAT?!
OH, NEVER MIND.
WE WERE HAPPY THEN, IN CASE YOU FORGOT.
KRAK

THAT WAS BEFORE I REALIZED THAT I DIDN'T WANT TO BE YOUR CLONE.
WOULD THAT HAVE BEEN SO BAD? DO YOU REALLY HATE ME THAT MUCH?

YOU NEVER ASKED ME WHAT I WANTED!
PLEASE. TO ROLL AROUND AND CATFIGHT OTHER GIRLS AT THE COUNTY FAIR, WHILE DRUNKEN IDIOTS HOPE A BOOB POPS OUTS.
HEY, THAT'S NOT WHAT—!
YOU KNOW THAT'S NOT WHAT HAPPENS. I HEADLINED THE BIGGEST AUDITORIUM IN THIS STATE WITH MY FRIENDS LAST NIGHT TO A SOLD-OUT CROWD EVEN WITH THE THREAT OF A NARNIA LEVEL SNOWSTORM HITTING.
COUNTY FAIR?!
AND MY TITS STAYED IN MY TOP THE WHOLE TIME.
IT'S DISGRACEFUL! WHAT YOU COULD'VE DONE. WHAT YOU COULD'VE BEEN!
I DON'T CARE WHAT YOU THINK.
WE HAD IT ALL PLANNED OUT!
PAGEANTS AND TALENT CONTESTS UNTIL YOUR TEENS. HOMESCHOOLED THE WHOLE TIME TO PREPARE YOU FOR THE NATIONAL BEAUTY PAGEANTS.
THAT'S WHERE THE MONEY, FAME AND SCHOLARSHIPS WOULD'VE STARTED ROLLING IN.
YOU WOULD'VE HAD OPTIONS IF YOU'D ONLY HAVE...
STUCK TO THE PLAN!

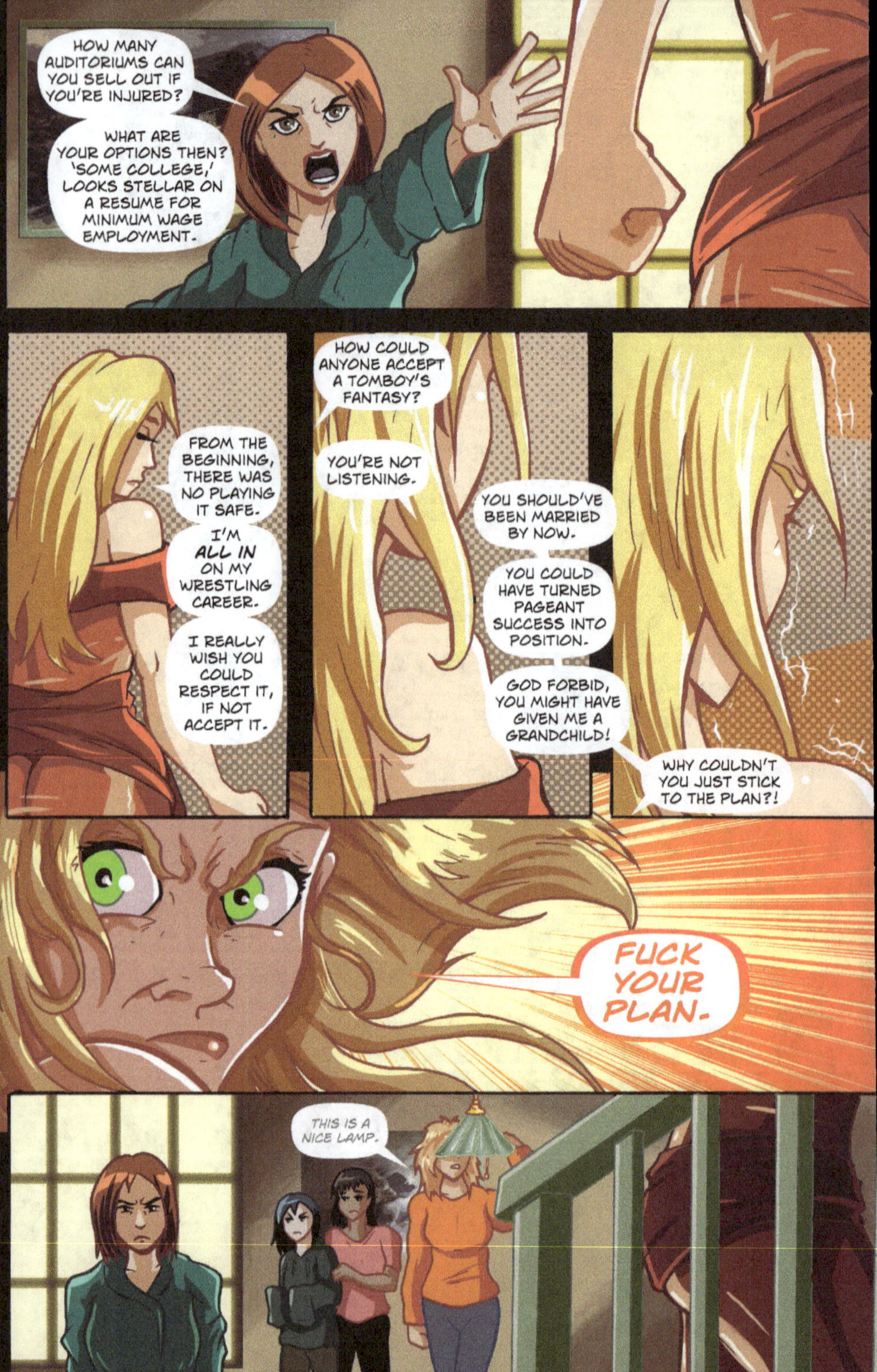

HOW MANY AUDITORIUMS CAN YOU SELL OUT IF YOU'RE INJURED?
WHAT ARE YOUR OPTIONS THEN? 'SOME COLLEGE,' LOOKS STELLAR ON A RESUME FOR MINIMUM WAGE EMPLOYMENT.
FROM THE BEGINNING, THERE WAS NO PLAYING IT SAFE.
I'M ALL IN ON MY WRESTLING CAREER.
I REALLY WISH YOU COULD RESPECT IT, IF NOT ACCEPT IT.
HOW COULD ANYONE ACCEPT A TOMBOY'S FANTASY?
YOU'RE NOT LISTENING.
YOU SHOULD'VE BEEN MARRIED BY NOW.
YOU COULD HAVE TURNED PAGEANT SUCCESS INTO POSITION.
GOD FORBID, YOU MIGHT HAVE GIVEN ME A GRANDCHILD!
WHY COULDN'T YOU JUST STICK TO THE PLAN?!
FUCK YOUR PLAN.
THIS IS A NICE LAMP.

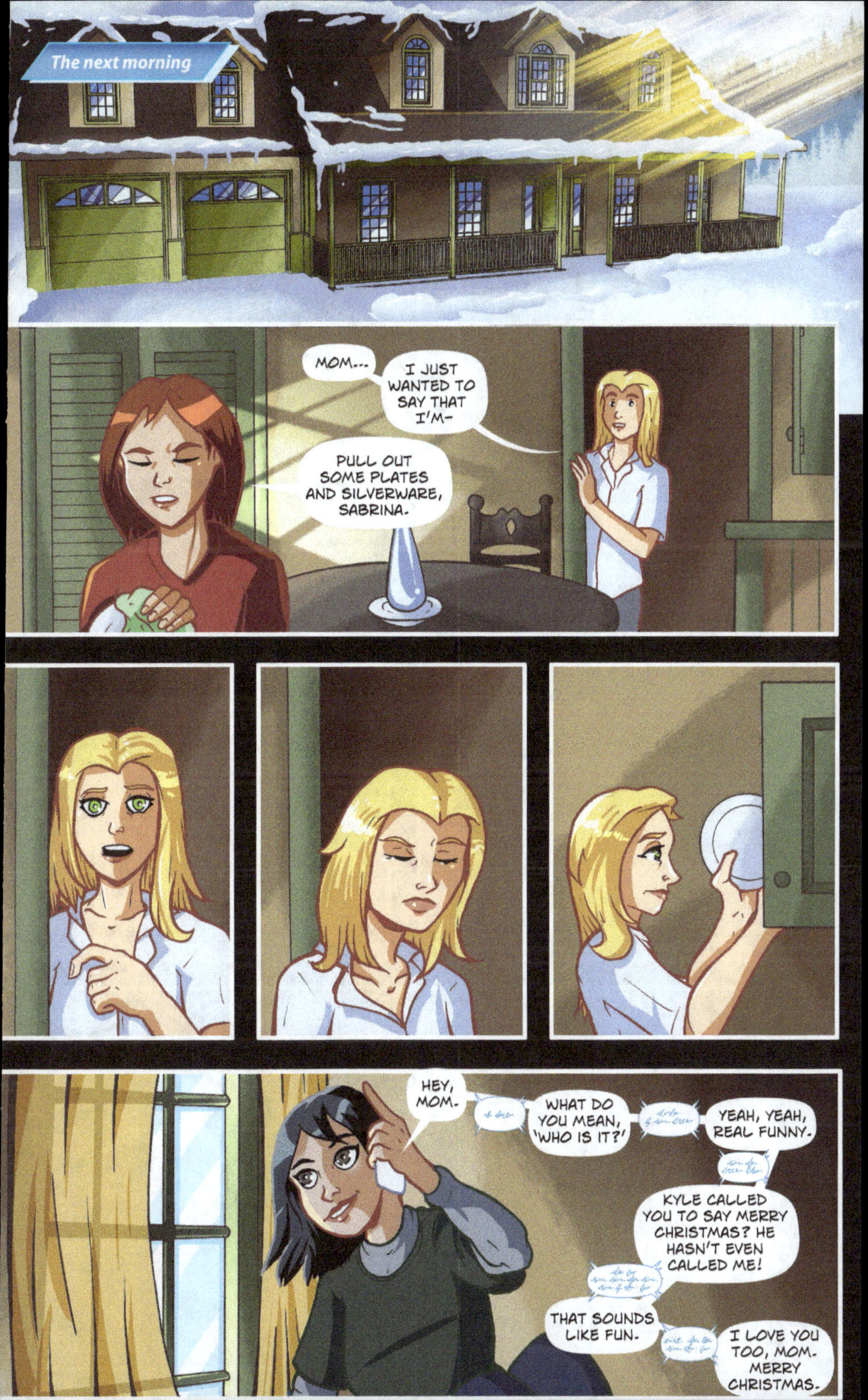

MOM...
I JUST WANTED TO SAY THAT I'M-
PULL OUT SOME PLATES AND SILVERWARE, SABRINA.

HEY, MOM.
WHAT DO YOU MEAN, 'WHO IS IT?'
YEAH, YEAH, REAL FUNNY.
KYLE CALLED YOU TO SAY MERRY CHRISTMAS? HE HASN'T EVEN CALLED ME!
THAT SOUNDS LIKE FUN.
I LOVE YOU TOO, MOM. MERRY CHRISTMAS.

IT LOOKS LIKE WE'LL BE LEAVING THIS MORNING.
THEY CLEARED THE RUNWAYS AND WE'LL BE FLYING OUT THIS AFTERNOON.

GOD, I MISS YOU GUYS.

HEY, MOM.
SORRY, I KNOW IT'S LATE.

IT'S OKAY, HONEY.
YOU LOOK BEAUTIFUL.

THANKS, MOM.

THE END

Acknowledgements

Special thanks to the Rival Angels readers!

KICKSTARTER

Kickstarter Sponsors and Patrons

Jim Payne
Brian Bishop
Peter Migala
Konstantine
Andrew McDonald
Bruce S. Fein
Matthew Peter Phaedonos
Tristrim "Comstar" Murnane
Daniel Monson
Ted Brown
Donald Cole
S.M.H

Ring Crew
To those that listen,
indulge, build up and support.

Aaron
Mabel
Kay
Lora
Justin
Tracie

NEXT IN
RIVAL
ANGELS

SECU
CURIT

www.ingramcontent.com/pod-product-compliance
Lightning Source LLC
Chambersburg PA
CBHW071126100726
47908CB00008B/2509